E. Davis

I0549357

THE LEGEND
OF
VISION
CAMPBELL

E. Davis

©Writers Block Publishing LLC

The characters in this book are fictitious; any resemblance to real persons living or dead is coincidental

Edited by Writers Block Publishing LLC

www.writersblockpublishingllc.com

www.edavisllc.com

writersblockpub@yahoo.com

1

I HAD NO IDEA that the many times I saw her, I was actually looking at her. Her beauty is a marvel; it's something to behold. She is the most beautiful woman in the world. She had light brown skin, and her eyes were the color of honey or liquid gold. Her copper-colored hair was worn like mine, in dread locks that had formed into ringlets called Goddess Locs. As reserved and set apart and private she likes to be, everyone on The Island has seen her because she is a model. Her face has and continues to grace the covers of magazines and billboards.

I had moved into a loft that she owned. I was renting it for the summer. I had never actually done business with her. She had sent one of her minions to have me sign a three-month lease. The minion looked at me, shocked when I gave her a check covering my stay for three months.

"What do you do, Ms. Calloway?" she asked.

"I'm an author," I answered.

She nodded her head, not in an approving way, but a way that simply said; Okay.

"What brings you to The Island?" the minion asked.

"Summer vacation, plus my godsons' christening," I answered with a smile.

I hoped that if I smiled, she would smile too; she didn't. As a matter of fact, she looked at me suspiciously as if I was hiding something as if I was not telling her enough information about my life. What more can I say? I am here with my best friend LaKeya Matthews and her husband Booker to christen their twin newborn sons, Isaiah and

David. LaKeya had wanted me to actually stay with her and Booker, but considering that they just had the twins, I felt like an intruder. She told me about the loft that *she,* the great beauty owned, and suggested that I rent it out during the summer.

"It's very expensive, Journey," she said to me.

"I have money," I reported.

LaKeya didn't reply.

So here I am renting this beautiful three-bedroom, a large Great Room, dining room, a kitchen, full bathroom, and looking at the minion wondering if there was anything else that she needed. She has my social security number. Why keep secrets?

I took a deep breath hoping that the minion didn't see that I was also running away from my pain, a failed relationship. If I hide on The Island, maybe he will forget about me, and maybe I will forget about him. Considering that I am here to forget about him, I will not mention him to The Minion. I continue to smile at her with hopes that she accepts my answer. After what seemed like twenty minutes, she stopped looking at me and then finally grinned.

"I hope this loft is to your liking." She said.

"Yes, it is perfect," I said.

The minion nodded her head and handed me a key.

"Thank you," I said.

"Fell free to decorate how you chose, paint the walls any color. If you have any questions, you call me, not her."

Why not her? I asked myself.

The fact that I plan to be here no longer than three months, it shouldn't matter if I met *her*, but the fact that I may never meet her intrigued me.

I stood still and watched The Minion leave. As she shuts the door, I walk to the small window that leads to the front of the yard and watch her walk away. Quickly, I walk to the front and lock the door. Then I realized she might have an extra key and come in whenever she feels like it. Suddenly, I hated her.

I unpacked my clothes and got settled. Afterward, I called LaKeya and told her that I have arrived in my new home.

"You must come over," she expressed.

I could tell that she was smiling. I can see her, lounging on the large white sofa, in a long silky white dress, with the windows open, allowing the cool air to baptize her.

I was not in the mood to visit at the moment, but I can tell in her voice that she wants company.

"Booker will send the car to come get you." She told me.

"Okay,"

I SIT IN THE back seat of the car that Booker sent for me and look at the scenery of The Island. The Island is beautiful. A tropical paradise full of affluent African-Americans that visit during the summer who want a change from Martha's Vineyard. The Island is full of rich people, from old money to new money. I am glad to see so many African-Americans, black people, doing well; Black Excellence. I saw the culture, the Black Culture. I saw afros, curly hair, braids, dreadlocks, head wraps. I saw the light-skinned, brown skin, brown skin, and dark brown

6

skin. I saw the older generation walk slowly along the streets holding their grandchildren's hands. The Island is heaven.

LaKeya warned me about The Island, that there is an issue with new money vs. old money. The old money is called The Established, and the new money is called; The New. LaKeya told me that The New constantly has to prove to The Established their worth. She also warned me about the never-ending issue with light-skinned blacks vs. dark-skinned blacks. As I sit in the back, I don't see light-skinned or dark-skinned. I don't see The New or The Established; I see a rich community.

LAKEYA AND BOOKER'S HOME, or I should say The Palace, is as big as Buckingham Palace. It looks like a castle—the mile-long driveway leading to the front gates, with the large M in the center. The Palace seemed magical. The kind that I saw in the fairy tale books. The marble stone water fountain in the center of the frontcourt. I saw servants, not housekeepers but servants in the frontcourt, tending to the area, sweeping the front end, tending to the rose garden, or just standing on post ready to take orders wearing tuxedos or black and white maid uniforms.

Booker's family comes from old money, The Established. They are bankers, one of a few black-owned banks in The United States of America. Their home back in the States is just as big as The Palace here on The Island.

AS THE DRIVER OPENS for me, LaKeya and Booker greet me smiling.

"Journey!" she says, with her arms open.

I run to her, and we hug each other. It's been a good two years since I saw LaKeya. I step back and look at her; she looks absolutely beautiful. Her light brown skin glistens under the bright sun. Her auburn-colored hair was in a bob hairstyle. She wears a tight, peach-colored lace dress—her make-up, natural, just a little mascara with soft burned orange-colored lips gloss.

"LaKeya, you look-," I tried to say. "I can't believe you just had twins."

She shrugged her shoulders in a blasé manner as if being beautiful is normal.

"You looked chic and stylish," she said to me.

I am a brown-skinned woman, with dark brown hair, almost black, with long dreadlocks. I wear a pair of navy blue wide-leg slacks a white short-sleeve button-up white shirt. My dreadlocks are pinned in a high bun, and I wear a pair of black platform peep toe high heels. For my jewelry, I wear a large silver cuff bracelet, a pair of silver and diamond teardrop earrings, and a white crystal pendant necklace.

I greeted Booker with a hug as well.

"Good to see you, Journey." Booker said, "Keya hasn't stopped talking about you all week. Congrats on the books!"

"Thank you, Booker," I said, smiling.

"Where are my godsons?" I asked.

"Finally asleep," Booker said, smiling.

Together we walk back into the house and through the long hallway to one of the sitting areas. The sitting area has a back door leading to a balcony that overlooks the tennis court and one of their pools. The sitting area includes two sofas, two love seats, coffee, and two end tables. The chandelier on the ceiling was made of pure crystal and gold. The room white with a few pictures of Booker's family members, no one living but great-great-grandparents. Also in the sitting room is a man, a handsome, dark-skinned black male. He stands as we enter the living room.

"Nathan Moore," LaKeya said smiling. "Meet my oldest and dearest friend, Journey Calloway. Journ, Nathan Moore, the boys' godfather."

Nathan approaches me with a grin. He looks good. He wears a pair of black slacks and a gray button-up shirt, his top button unbuttoned. His hair was cut low, and he had a goat-tee, and his eyes are dark and piercing. I don't know if I should fear him or fall in love.

"The writer," Nathan said, shaking my head.

"Nice to meet you," I say.

I can see LaKeya standing behind Nathan with a smile on her face. She wanted me here to link up with Nathan. I must admit that he is very handsome, and the sudden ambush is somewhat exciting, if not scary, but I am not in the exact mood to be on a date or be involved in some kind of romantic setup. I was hoping to spend time with LaKeya, watch Booker drink scotch or brandy, and listen to him talk about his family's wealth. I want to spend time with my godsons by trying to figure out which one is Isaiah and which one is David and eat large colossal shrimp and large scallops soaked in butter and garlic, oh, and of course drink.

"Dinner will be served shortly," said one of the butlers.

"What's on the menu?" I asked.

"Scallops, lobster, and steak." The butler answered.

I grinned at Nathan and think, maybe I can do those things, spend time with my godsons, spend time with LaKeya, and maybe spend time with Nathan.

"Tell me how things are in Pittsburgh," LaKeya said, handing me a glass of Champaign. "Do they miss me yet?"

I chuckled at her vanity, and her out-of-touch questioned, considering that she and I haven't lived in Pittsburgh since college. I went to NYU to study writing, and she went to Morehouse to study sociology and how to be a rich man's wife. Although we are from Pittsburgh, we don't visit. We both live in New York, in Manhattan, me in the city, Booker and she in the suburbs. Our families moved from Pittsburgh. My parents and LaKeya's parents live in Atlanta.

"My mother hasn't mentioned anything new," I said, sipping my Champaign.

"Keya, Pittsburgh is not so bad," Booker said, handing Nathan a glass of brandy.

"Please," LaKeya said, rolling her eyes. "Pittsburgh is not known for supporting us or anyone else, just steel and the Steelers."

"The Steelers are a good team," Nathan said, smiling. "Plus great schools, Carnegie Mellon, Point Park."

I grinned.

"What do you do, Nathan?" I ask.

"A sports agent," Nathan said.

I nod my head.

"What new adventure are you writing?" Booker asked.

"I just released my latest book," I answered. "Maybe being on The Island will give me some ideas."

"How many books does your publisher require of you?" Nathan asked.

"She's independent," LaKeya said. "She has no publisher,"

I look at LaKeya. Her comment sounded as if I had no home, no hope, that I was Literary Orphan. I smile at Nathan.

"I work for myself, not a publisher. I'm self-published." I explained.

"Must be nice," Nathan said. "Not having to be under a contract. Working completely for yourself."

I nod my head.

"It is. I am under no one's contract; I write as often as I want to, bring in the royalties, and live the dream."

I raise my glass. Booker and Nathan raise their glasses with me, but LaKeya just grinned.

"It is great," Booker said. "I am glad that my family established a business, so I have a place to come to. I don't have to fill out a job application or submit a resume with hopes of a callback. I grew up in the business. All I needed to do was just study a few things about money and business, and here I am."

He raises his glass. Nathan, LaKeya, and I raised our glasses too.

"A lot of people don't teach our children how to manage money or how to start a business and to leave legacies to our children," Nathan said.

"What if the boys don't want to go into banking?" I asked.

"I thought of that," Booker said. "I want them to be happy, if they want to join a circus, I would be supportive, but I want them to know that there is an establishment for them."

"A circus, Booker, you can't be serious," LaKeya said, rolling her eyes. "My sons are going to be great. They can doctors, lawyers, businessmen, not lion tamers or acrobats."

I chuckle as I sip my drink. LaKeya has always been about image. I know that it would not benefit the Matthews family for their newest members to be in a circus. If they did not grow up to be socially refined, it would kill them. As LaKeya talks about how princely her sons will be, I begin to imagine them lying in their little cribs wearing baby Argyle onesies and matching booties.

DINNER WAS SERVED IN the garden. As humid as it is on The Island, the air at Booker and LaKeya's is surprisingly cool and comforting unless I had forgiven the humidity because I was eating lobster and scallops with steamed broccoli and rice pilaf. It was a simple dinner to most people, but elegant with the pretty white table cloth over the table, beautiful white dinner china with floral prints on them, and coral-colored dinner napkins. The lightning from the sunset makes the scenery look almost epic, as if this was a beautiful fairy tale. Although everything looks like a portrait, it's real; we're real. I find myself laughing and talking about life, from politics to business to children.

"LaKeya, remember when we were young, and my mom took us to see Janet Jackson! And her car broke down!"

I laugh as I try to tell the story. LaKeya rolls her eyes and chuckles, to the assumption to relive the moment with me.

"So, the engine was overheating! And Miss LaKeya here was a die-hard Janet Jackson fan! She had to get to this concert! She had on her black Rhythm Nation outfit, a key earring, the key for LaKeya right. So the car was smoking, and the engine was not trying to turn! Miss LaKeya here went to the hood of the car and was trying to blow on the engine!"

I laugh so hard at the flashback.

"I have to see Janet," I said, imitating LaKeya. "My mom shook her head at LaKeya, 'baby, the car is dead,' "She told her. "

I watch Booker and Nathan laugh with me.

"' The car is dead!', "She screamed as if she witnesses a homicide!"

Booker, Nathan, and I laughed. I think it was funny because of how refined and demure LaKeya is now. As I laugh, I look at LaKeya and see the cool look on her face, as if my trip down memory lane does not amuse her.

"Key," I said, smiling.

She shrugs her shoulders coolly as if she is too cool to laugh with us.

"Your mother was known to come up short," LaKeya said. "Christmas time, the stove was broke, so we traveled up the street in the snow carrying a turkey in a roaster, asking the neighbors to help cook."

She shakes and her head as if the act was appalling. I shrug my shoulders.

"Well, to better days," I said as I hold my Champaign glass up. "Started from the bottom and now we are here,"

"Now, we're here!" Nathan is smiling, joining my toast.

Suddenly Nathan's cell phone rings. He pulls the phone from his pocket to look at who is calling him.

"Excuse me," Nathan said, standing up.

I watch as Nathan walks away from the table. Then one of the servants comes to the table.

"Mr. Matthews," said the servant. "You have a phone call."

I watch as LaKeya shoots him a look.

"You're having dinner," LaKeya admonishes.

"Just a few moments," Booker said with a grin. "Journ, excuse me."

I watch as Booker stands and quickly walks into the house to take the phone call. I look at LaKeya. I wonder what is going through her mind. She has always been somewhat uptight, but right now, she is acting stuck up, as if she is too good for conversation. She seems frustrated with Booker. I look at her left hand. Her wedding ring is 18 karat.

"You okay, Key?" I ask. "You seem tense."

"I'm fine," she said quickly; she sips her wine.

"Key, how many glasses can you have? Aren't you nursing?"

"God no." she scoffs. "I don't have time to nurse *twins*."

"What about the bonding? The mommy and sons time." I said.

14

"There are two babies, not one. Soon as I nurse one, the other is hungry, and the cycle repeats its self." She shakes her head at the thought. "Besides, how much bonding will I do with boys anyway?"

"What do you mean?" I chuckle. "You are their first lady to them. You set the tone to how they treat women."

"The boys women raise still end up like their father." She rolls her eyes. "Love what life brings instead of the women that bear them life."

I take in a deep breath. She looks away. I notice that tears well up in her eyes.

"I prayed that my boys be slow will never marry."

"Key," I gasp. "What's the matter?"

Is this Postpartum Depression? She gets up from the table and walks to the edge of the backyard. I follow her.

"Don't get me wrong, Journ," she begins. "I love my boys. I am happy to have healthy and beautiful baby boys."

"You and Booker okay?" I asked.

"Yes, but he's always so busy! The bank, the bank, the bank, never me."

I nod my head.

"Everything will be okay," I said, rubbing her back. "He's a businessman."

"We have old money, Journey," LaKeya said. "We are The Established."

I didn't have the heart to ask if there is someone else. If I ask myself that question out loud, then I would

have to wonder and to think if there is a possibility and it may be true, that my friend who is like my brother, is stepping out on my friend, my sister. Booker doesn't seem the type. He smiles at LaKeya, not just a friendly smile, but a smile that says that he loves her. I stand up straight, with hopes that my friend didn't feel my concern or worry or mentally hear my thoughts.

"Key, Book is a businessman. He's in charge of family money; The Established money." I said.

She looks at me; her mahogany-colored eyes were smiling. I smiled at her.

"We are a long way from those Projects, girl," I said.

"You're a long way," she said, "You are a successful woman. I am a rich man's wife."

"Regardless of how we got to live like George and Weezie, we here! We didn't have to sell drugs or our dignity to get here."

"You right, Journ." She said. "I am so glad you here?"

"Always here for you."

I watch her take in a deep breath.

"I'm going to wash my face and change my clothes."

"Okay," I said.

I watch her leave. I returned to my seat at the table and reunited with my scallops and shrimps. Nathan returns to the table.

"Where is everyone?" he asked.

"Booker had a phone call, and Key wanted to change clothes."

Nathan chuckles.

"Those two."

"What?"

"She changes clothes three times a day, morning, noon, and then dinner," Nathan said. "She is the lady of the house, you know. She does it to get Booker's attention."

I shrug.

"That's what we do," I said in a flirtatious manner. "We are peacocks. We want the men to notice us. Men are those deer and moose with those large antlers trying to get the women's attention."

I chuckle.

"I just compared men and women to animals, didn't I?"

Nathan chuckles.

"It's better than that Venus and Mars theory," Nathan said.

As we sit and finish eating, I see an airplane flying by carrying a banner. Nathan looks up and then shakes his head.

"What?" I asked.

"Her, she is so obvious." Nathan said. "That peacock makes it very clear."

"What?" I asked.

Nathan looks at me. His eyes are shocked that I know nothing about what he is talking about. My eyes grew intense, questioning what he is talking about.

"Keya, the peacock?" I asked.

"No, Booker's ex-girlfriend," Nathan said. "That was her plane flying by. She tries to get his attention."

I let out a nervous chuckle. Maybe there is another woman.

"Who is she?" I asked. "The other woman."

Nathan looks at me, and then quickly, he sits back.

"I said too much." He said.

"No, you didn't say quite enough. You telling me that Booker is cheating on Keya?" I interrogate.

"I don't know for sure," Nathan said. "I just know that ever since he and LaKeya got together and married, her face is everywhere, especially on The Island. She is The New. So she had a lot more to prove."

I shake my head at that old money, new money concept.

"Why does she have a lot more to prove because of her financial status?" I asked.

"Because The New has to prove to The Established that they are not here by a fluke," Nathan said. "You have to prove yourself as an independent writer."

"I don't have to prove anything. I have money. I worked hard for my money. I don't care what people think of me. I know my worth." I said.

"Me too," Nathan said.

"So, what are the issues with the ex-girlfriend?" I asked.

"No need to get gangsta." Nathan joked. "She just wants Booker to see what he is missing."

I laugh. I finish my scallop and finish my drink. I shake my head.

"Women are silly," I said.

Nathan chuckles.

"Have you done anything to get your ex's attention?" He asked.

I look away. I don't want to talk about my ex. I don't know this man well enough to discuss my relationships. I look at Nathan.

"Have you?" I pressed.

"I didn't build my success to prove to society that I am worth their admiration," Nathan said. "But I must admit that if I ran into an ex that dropped me because I was not enough, and now they see me. I admit my pride will steps in to say, 'Look at me now,'."

I nod.

"I can see that," I reply.

"That is what she did," Nathan said. "Booker loved her, but his family said that she is not enough. So she took that and made herself enough. And now, every summer when LaKeya and Booker is here, she shows up in a very obvious yet subtle way."

I shrug.

I look at the scenery. The sun had set, and the sky is a beautiful navy blue. There are no stars and no moon, but there is beauty in the plain sky.

"I'm going to change the subject," I said with a grin.

"Okay," Nathan said.

"We are godparents," I said. "What can we do as godparents for the boys to know that we are here?"

"Besides buy them every toy their parents won't. Take them to the club when they are twenty-one." Nathan jokes.

I chuckle.

"Men," I said, laughing. "What about school, education."

"With Booker's money, there is no school they can't get in," Nathan said.

"Okay, so our goal as godparents is to make sure they are not-," I begin.

"Rotten mutha-,"

"Nathan!" I admonish and then laugh.

He laughs with me. I notice that he has a beautiful smile.

Booker and LaKeya return together smiling. Holding hands like Barak and Michelle. I smile at them. I wink at her. She looks beautiful. She wear a pair of wide legged cream colored pants and cream silk sleeveless shirt with a beautiful cream kimono with pink and soft yellow roses on it. I watch them as they sit down. Servants come to remove our plates.

"Dessert?" they ask.

"Journey, we have of course cheesecake. Chocolate Moose," LaKeya said smiling.

"Baby," Booker interrupts. "She had to try Andrea's peach cobbler."

"Oh yes!" LaKeya says smiling. "Monte, bring us some of that cobbler."

"Yes ma'am."

"Cobbler, servants, and scallops-," I begin.

"Oh my," Nathan says smiling.

LAKEYA WALKS ME TO the car. The driver waiting for us, our arms are linked together; sisters. The air is surprisingly cool, it feels good.

"So you and Book okay?" I ask.

"Yes." She said. "I looked at my handsome beautiful boys and realized that all is well." She answers.

"Good." I said.

"It's nice to see you and Nathan getting along so well." She said, in a prying type of way.

"No, no." I said, breaking away from her arms.

"What?" LaKeya asked suspiciously.

20

"Listen, I am doing me this summer. Enjoying living on The Island and sitting with the bourgeois sipping on tea."

LaKeya laughs at me.

"You don't like tea." She scoffs.

"No, but to sit with them with my pearls, I will pretend like I do," I said, smiling at her.

"Nathan is a good man and rich," LaKeya said.

"I am a good woman and rich. Key, I have my own money. I don't need a man for money. I need a man for companionship. Besides, we live in two different states, two different types of jobs and lives."

"You're a writer," LaKeya said. "You can pick up your laptop and move."

"Ha-ha," I said. "I know that, but seriously Key, I am not trying to meet no one. I'm doing me."

"Okay," LaKeya said, shrugging to surrender. "Tomorrow morning, I come get you, and we shop until we are stupid."

"Sound like a plan," I said, laughing.

We say goodbye, kissing each other on the cheek.

The driver holds the door open for me. As I get inside, I look at LaKeya.

"I can get use to this." I said to her.

"Good, I will be picking you up early, ten a.m."

And then the door shuts. I sit back in my seat, buckle my seat belt.

2

I WAKE UP TO, pretty colorful birds singing outside my window. Quickly I walk to the window and watch as the pretty candy-colored birds fly, sing and play together. It must have rained because I smell fresh wet grass. I close my eyes and inhale. I am enjoying what is in front of me. I wonder what I life would be if I take up residency on The Island. As I look at the sun that has already reached the highest level in the sky, I think of the books I can write on The Island, I think of all of the inspirations that may come to me. I slowly walk around the bedroom. It's large. The walls are white; the large king-size bed has a gold headboard; the sheets are made with that five-thousand count thread. I don't remember closing my eyes or laying down my head. I just remember waking up feeling rested. The floor is made of a maroon-colored cedar room. The vanity in the front of the room is pure ivory with gold handles. I wonder how rich is Vision Campbell, but then I shake my head because that fact is moot.

As I shower, the water feels so good against my skin. I watch the waterfall from the showerhead; it looks as like diamond dust falling. The bathroom is just a lovely as the bedroom. The large bathroom is the colors of gold and cream, the faucets on the sink and the tub are pure gold. The walls are the color of cream, the floor cream color marble. The bathroom makes me think of heaven, with the streets of gold. I wonder if Vision Campbell thought of heaven when she had the bathroom design. Inside the bathroom, there is a Jacuzzi-style bathtub; I'm looking forward to soaking in that tub this summer. The standing shower has three showerheads that operate by voice activation. Vision's Minion told me to set my voice using a four numeric code, and when I leave after the summer, I will be able to deactivate the voice command using the same numeric code. Also in the bathroom is a toilet and a bidet. When I first saw the bathroom, I shook my head.

Who spends this much time in the bathroom? I asked myself.

However, after my first night here and now my first morning, I may spend some quality time in this Bathroom Spa.

I HEAR LAKEYA HONK the horn outside. I shake my head.

She honking for me like I'm her date, a bad date; I shook my head, looking out of the window of the breakfast nook. I continue to sip my coffee and look at her through the window. Her car is a pearl-colored Maybach. She honks the horn again. I chuckle and take a bite out of my toast. I watch her from the window; she gets out of the car, storms to the front door, and rings the doorbell.

Slowly I stand and then slowly walk to the front door and open it. LaKeya stands in front of me on the opposite side of the storm door. She has her hands on her hips, and her brown eyes are piercing into me as she looks at me scornfully. LaKeya looks beautiful. She is wearing a mustard yellow sleeveless sundress with emerald-colored flowers at the bottom of the dress. I see a beautiful gold cuff bracelet on her left arm. LaKeya wears gold and diamond hoop-style earrings, and her necklace is a thin gold necklace. Her bob-style hair shines under the sun.

"Good morning, Key. Would you like to come in?" I ask.

"No, didn't you hear me honking the horn?" she questions.

"I did, but I don't just run outside as if you a bad date," I said. "Besides, I am eating a quick breakfast. Come in?"

I open the door to welcome LaKeya in. Reluctantly, she enters and follows me into the breakfast nook. I can tell that she is impressed, but she doesn't want to admit to it.

"This home is beautiful," I said. "Would you like some coffee?"

"No," she answered. "We have all day,"

"So why rush?" I said, sitting down. "Relax,"

She signs and sits down across from me. I look at her from the side of my eye with a small grin with hopes to get that sour disposition off her face. Eventually, she gives in and smiles.

"Relax," I said, rolling my eyes. "We are on vacation. There is no structured time. We can do what we want."

"Whatever," LaKeya says, rolling her eyes. "You look nice today."

"Thank you," I say in my English accent.

She laughs at me. I wear a pair of black Capri slacks and a white sleeveless button-up shirt. I wear my dreads in a ponytail, and I wear a pair of silver hoop earrings. I didn't expect LaKeya to be so formal when it came to a shopping spree, but then again, I should have known better, considering that she is married to a very rich banker. Every day is a fashion show with her. I am technically under dressed, but as much as I love clothes, I refuse to parade around The Island in a thousand-dollar designer clothes with the humidity.

"You look rich," I said.

She smiles that snobbish smile. I finish my coffee and eat the last of my toast.

"Are you ready?" she questions.

"Yes, yes, let me get my purse!" I said.

I walk out of the breakfast nook to get my little crossover bag; I slide on my flats and clear my throat.

"I'm ready," I say in my English accent.

Quickly LaKeya gets up and walks to the front door. She opens the door and storms to her Phantom. I chuckle and walk out the loft and lock the door. In the car, I buckle up as she races off.

"This is a nice car, Key," I say, looking around.

"Thank you," she smiles. "Booker gave it to me as a push gift."

"A Phantom?" I question. "A push gift is jewelry, not a car."

"I gave birth to twins, so I get a car. You want jewelry; it's pearl-colored."

I chuckle as I shake my head.

"You are going to love the shops on The Island." She says. "Everything shop is upscale and chic. We'll go to the places you can afford."

"I can afford it?" I ask. "Excuse me?"

She looks at me.

"I don't mean that-,"

"Just because I don't bath in money doesn't mean that I don't have any," I said to her.

"How rich can you be? You are self-published, and your sales are solely on Amazon." She scoffs.

I take a deep breath. LaKeya doesn't value my worth. As I sit inside her beautiful Maybach car, with the white and gold interior, I never thought that my best friend would not consider me successful. We come from the same hood, the same background. Both our parents were blue-collar; we live in the same ghetto neighborhood. We were neighbors and best friends. She may have been a little more refined than my family that is because my family did not need the validation of others to feel better about their lives. However, at this moment, I feel that I need LaKeya's validation. I have never been the kind of person that needed validation. I shake my head at her comment, not feeling the need to justify it. I am going to believe that she didn't mean it the way it sounded.

THE FIRST PLACE OF shopping we stop at is a beautiful boutique called Christina's, owned by an African woman named Christina. Her boutique is beautiful; as I enter in, immediately I am hit with the fresh smell of lavender. I see mannequins wearing fine silks and beautiful jewelry, the type of jewelry that Elizabeth Taylor wore. The boutique is made of glass; everyone can see inside. The marble floor colors are various grays, from smoky gray to a very light, almost white-colored gray.

"LaKeya," I hear someone say.

LaKeya smiles at me,

"That's Christina!" LaKeya says, smiling at me.

A woman quickly approaches us; her beauty is blinding. She has rich colored brown skin and round eyes

26

that is decorated with blue and white eye-shadow forcing those almond-colored eyes to pop. She wore a white pantsuit with a sapphire and diamond pendant necklace. Surprisingly she wears her hair straight with light brown and blond highlights. Her smile is electrifying. I can't help but smile back.

"Christina, meet my friend, Journey-,"

"Calloway, yes!" Christina said, extending her hand to me.

"Hello," I smile as I shake her hand.

"It is a pleasure to meet you. I am a big fan of your work." She said, smiling.

"Thank you," I said, smiling. "Your boutique is beautiful!"

"Thank you," Christina said, smiling.

"LaKeya, how are you and those twins?" Christina asks, smiling.

"They are well," LaKeya said, smiling. "We need to get something special for their Christening."

"Yes," Christina said. "It is the talk of The Island."

"Oh?" LaKeya questioned.

"Oh yes, those handsome babies," Christina said.

"Well, Journey is the godmother, and she needs something just as special," LaKeya said.

Christina nods her head.

"Yes, come this way."

Together we follow Christina to the back of the boutique. I watch as LaKeya walks. She walks with her head held high. Her demeanor is regal. As I watch her, I grin.

"She is taking us to the V.I.P. suite." LaKeya whispers.

"V.I.P?" I ask.

"Yes," Christina says to me. "Only the privileged are welcome back here. That is The Established and a selected few of The New."

I take in a deep breath.

"I am of The Established," LaKeya said as Christina unlock a door.

Together the three of us enter inside the pretty, all-white room. It is one of the many rooms that are not surrounded by glass—there white plush, wall-to-wall carpet, a white sofa, and two love seats. A glass coffee table white a dozen of white roses with lavender flowers as fillers. There is a large bay window that has a view of the ocean.

"Have a seat," Christina said, smiling.

I follow LaKeya's lead. She walks to the couch and takes a seat. I sit beside her. Then two ladies enter, one carrying a bucket of Champaign and the other with caviar. I look at LaKeya. She holds her head up high and smiles at me.

"See what I am teaching you." She says to me.

I grin.

What you are teaching me? I ask myself.

I wonder if she remembers that last time we were together in Atlanta, and she and I were at a country club dining on caviar and Champaign while our then boyfriends were golfing on the golf course.

Then two other ladies enter in with a rack of clothes.

"Those are beautiful," I said.

28

One of the ladies hands me a glass of Champaign. I take it, take a quick sip, and then set my glass down to look at the rack of clothing. I almost gasp when I feel the material, silks that are softer than silks. I look at Christina; she smiles at me. I look back at LaKeya.

"Everything is so beautiful." I said to her.

"Oh yes," LaKeya said, walking to the rack.

"Christina, I want something with an island vibe," I said. "You know, maybe I can wrap my locks up in a beautiful silk scarf, maybe-,"

"You will not stand as the godmother to my boys looking like some kind of bama."

"Excuse me?" I said. "African queens are known to wear head wraps."

"Oh yes, the most elegant queens," Christina said, smiling. "Journey, I see you in purple, maybe emerald green."

I close my eyes and imagine myself wearing a beautiful purple and gold headscarf that is shaped on my head like a crown. I see myself wearing a beautiful gown with bright colors, from the purples, the greens, the blues, and the yellows. I am holding my beautiful godsons, one in each arm, as I promise to love them. Aunt Journey will always make sure that these young kings will be well-rounded.

"Journey!" LaKeya says my name, pulling me from my trance.

"Yes," I said.

I hold an emerald-colored green dress, strapless with a long handkerchief bottom half. I look at Christina, and she smiles at me.

"I think you and Nathan should wear something similar, considering that you two are the godparents."

I nod my head thinking of LaKeya's idea.

"This is not a wedding, Key. I am not a bridesmaid, and he is not a groomsman wearing a matching boutonniere."

"I know, but it would be nice if there is some kind of coordination," LaKeya said.

"Then tell Nathan, I want to wear this ocean blue dress," I said, pulling the dress from the rack.

"Oh, that is beautiful," Christina said, smiling.

The dress is beyond beautiful. It was the color of blue topaz—a sleeveless A-line dress, with sapphire and onyx jewels at the bottom.

"I need this dress, Christina," I said. "Tell Nathan; this is what I am wearing."

LaKeya shakes her head.

"I don't know, Journ."

I don't respond to her. There is a dressing room in the white room. Quickly I enter the dressing room.

"Journ!" LaKeya calls my name.

"LaKeya, try this beautiful dress on," Christina said. "It is your color."

In the dressing room, I quickly remove my clothes and try on the dress. I come of the room, needing assistance with zipping the back of the dress: Christina and her help gasps at how pretty it looks. Quickly I walk to the mirror and smile at the pretty dark-skinned woman smiling back at me.

"I love this dress!" I exclaim.

"Perfect," Christina says,

I feel her pulling at the back of the dress. It is a bit lose in the front around the bust line.

"Allow me to take this in for you. I will have it delivered." Christina said.

"Okay," I said, smiling.

"Where are you staying?" One of Christina's help asks.

"I'm staying on Indigo Ave," I answered.

"Vision Campbell's loft?" Christina asks.

"Yes," I answered.

"Oh, that loft is amazing." Said the help.

"I know!" I exclaimed.

LaKeya comes out of the dressing room. She looks beautiful in the dress that Christina had picked for her. It is a coral-colored empire-style dress. With her bob hair style, she looks like a Greek goddess. The gold cuff that she wears, I can see one on her bicep. I smile at LaKeya.

"You look good, girl!" I say.

"You look Obama Glam." She jokes.

Everyone laughs.

"So you know, Vision Campbell?" I ask. "Christina, have you dressed her?"

Christina looks away with a coy smile, which I took as a yes; she does know Vision Campbell.

"What is she like?" I ask.

No one wants to answer me. I look at them, hoping that I hear some juice on Vision Campbell. I didn't need to hear bad or negative gossip. I just want to know is she as beautiful as they say she is, but no one wants to comment. I take the hint and not say anything else about Vision Campbell, but now I am more intrigued with her.

I pay for my dress with cash.

LAKEYA AND I GO to another boutique. This time, shoes. As we ride down the street, I look at the sights. The Island is so beautiful. It looks almost magical.

"Where did you get all that cash?" LaKeya asks.

"What do you mean?" I ask, shocked by her question.

"Where did you get that money?"

"Key, I am a writer," I said.

"Writers don't make that kind of money," LaKeya comments as shaking her head. "Plus, you're not signed to anyone."

I take in a deep breath. LaKeya does not value my worth.

"LaKeya, I don't need to be signed to some kind of publisher to be financially successful," I said to her. "I work hard with my marketing, with my promoting, with my networking."

She rolls her eyes and shrugs her shoulders. I want to scream. I want to shake her.

"You market on social media. That is not real marketing."

"That is the way to market!" I snap. "I have a great following. I do speaking engagements and do seminars and workshops on how to build your brand!"

LaKeya chuckles. She is laughing at me as I try to explain my value to her. I shake my head.

"You're new money. That Kardashian Money. Making your money on appearances." She said. "That's a fad. That will go away when people are tired of you."

"That is why it's important to stay relevant," I said.

"How do you stay relevant? What do you do?"

"Write more books!" I snap. "I am a business!"

"Okay, okay," LaKeya said with a chuckle. "I was shocked that you hand all that cash to pay for that gown."

Meanwhile you put it on your tab, have the bill sent to Booker to pay, I say to myself.

"Well, I am of The New, and I here because I am Established."

"Well, okay," LaKeya said.

I can tell that she is mocking me, but I chose not to engage.

WE ENTER IN THE, shoe store. Like Christina, it is an elegant boutique that smells like fresh flowers. Unlike Christina's, the boutique is not made out of glass. There is a large bay window, with shoes displayed in the window. The walls were white, and there is a crystal chandelier. I smile as I enter the beautiful shoe store. The shoe store is run by a name Thom. As LaKeya and I enter the shoe store, Thom approaches us smiling! He is a tall, thin, lanky man light-skinned man with dark hair that is worn in thin small dreadlocks. He wears silver, whirred-rimmed glass. I smile at him. He is handsome. He smiles back. He wears a pair of black slacks and a black button-up shirt.

"Journey Calloway," he said my name.

"Hello," I reply, quickly shooting LaKeya a look.

"I am a big fan! I love your book, *The Mystery of the Sun*!" he said.

"Why thank you," I said.

"I'm Thom." He introduces, extending his hand. "Lady, Sandy, look who is on The Island."

Immediately, two women come from the back. They are a beautiful woman. One light-skinned and the other dark-skinned, both ladies wearing their hair in dreadlocks, both of them long dreadlocks. One whose locks look like goddess locks that hung down her back, and the other woman, her locks were pinned up into a bun. Both ladies smile at me; I smiled back.

"Hi," they both said, smiling at me.

"I'm Sandy," the light-skinned woman introduced.

"I'm Lauren, but Thom calls me Lady." The other woman said to me. "We are fans of your work! We follow you on Instagram!"

"Cool!" I said, smiling.

"LaKeya," Thom said smiling, "You did not tell us you know Journey Calloway."

LaKeya shrugs her shoulders.

"I didn't know you were fans of hers." She said.

"Who isn't?" Thom said.

"She isn't, apparently." I admonish. "I am looking for some spectacular shoes! Carrie Bradshaw style."

"Come this way," Thom said.

Together we follow Thom to his display of shoes. Like Christina's dresses, everything is sitting open on display stands looking elegant and beautiful. There are shoes beyond the Louboutin Shoes, Jimmy Choo, or Chanel, but shoes with diamond and crystal-covered heels. I saw glass slippers just like in *Cinderella,* clear glass and colored glass. Shoes with gemstones, pure gold, and silver on the buckles, these shoes were made of fine leather, silks, and suede. I drool at the beauty of the shoes. I am not a shoe whore, but to put a pair of these lovely shoes on my feet, I just might become a bit whorish.

"Please sit down," Thom said to me, pointing to an empty leather chair.

Feeling like a well-respected guess, I sit down in the chair. LaKeya sits next to me. I smile at her, excited and

34

feeling honored at the treatment Thom and his staff gives me. She smiles at me with a cool and prideful smile as if this treatment is normal and I am new to everything. Thom kneels before me as his ladies stand behind him, one on his left and the other on his right. I look at them; they smile at me. Thom holds his hand out to me for me to place my foot in his hand. Gently, I place my right foot into his left hand, and he holds my foot sweetly. He caresses my foot, gently enough to not tickle me and gentle enough for me to smile at him, hoping that this was an appropriate yet seductive move. As Lady gives him a pair of black leather five-inch platform shoes with a diamond and crystal-covered heel, I gasp. Then slowly, Thom put the shoe on my foot. I flex my foot and let out a sigh.

"Oh, my, god!" I say slowly.

"Yes," Thom asks.

I lean my head back and sigh. The ecstasy of this moment is beyond arousing. If there is any more touching of the feet and sliding on of the shoe, I would have had an orgasm in front of Thom, in front of his ladies, in front of LaKeya, and in front of the beautiful shoes and not cared. Thom places the other shoe on my foot. He helps me stand, and I feel like a beautiful exotic woman of the Amazon's; ironically, I am on The Island feeling like I am of The Island.

"They are you," Sandy said, smiling.

"Walk, Journey," Thom said.

I feel like I am some kind of Evangelical revival, and I have been given the miracle to walk. With everyone watching me, I put one foot in front of the other and glide across the showroom floor. Like at some kind of Evangelical revival, everyone cheers for me, as if me walking in these shoes was some kind of Pentecostal Miracle.

"I love them," I said, looking at LaKeya.

She nods her head, approvingly I hope. I nod my head, indicating I want these shoes.

"I will need a matching handbag," I said.

"Done!" Lady replies quickly.

I see her rush to the back of the store. I step out of the shoes and hand them to Thom to put back into a box. He nods his head.

"My turn," LaKeya said.

I sit down next to LaKeya, and she quickly sticks her foot out with hopes that Thom would caress her as I have done, but he holds her foot gently, and Sandy hands him a pair of gold shoes with crystal heels.

"Why are you not holding me like you held her?" LaKeya asks.

"Because you are someone's wife," Thom said, smiling.

"How do you know she doesn't have a man?" LaKeya questioned.

"Key, really?" I ask. "Is this really a competition on whose feet get caressed?"

LaKeya rolls her eyes. She sits up in the seat and then stands to walk in her shoes. I smile at her.

"Looks good, girl!" I encourage. "Perfect for your dress."

She shrugs her shoulders.

"I'll take them," she says to Thom.

"Very well, ladies."

Together, LaKeya and I follow Thom to purchase our shoes. Like before, I pay with cash.

"Journey, can we meet up while you are here on The Island. I have friends that have read your work and would love to meet you and spend some time with you." Thom asks.

"I would love that," I said, smiling. "What an honor."

I wrote down my email address.

LAKEYA AND I SIT in a beautiful restaurant. We sit outside on deck; although the air is humid, there is a breeze flowing through. The sun is high, and there is not a cloud in the sky. The tropical trees are beautiful. I see candy-colored birds flying around aimlessly without a care in the world.

"This is the life, LaKeya." I said, eating a piece of shrimp. "Just think, ten years ago, if someone told us that we be here on this beautiful island, we would have laughed."

"You laugh." She said, stabbing her fork into her salad. "I know that I would be here one day."

I have to admit, she is right. LaKeya has always had her eyes on the prize. We grew up in a small section in Pittsburgh. She and I were poor, living in the projects. We became best friends because our parents kept us apart from becoming a product of our environment. LaKeya and I were not allowed out of the house while our parents worked, and when we were out and about with other friends, we had to be home long before the street lights came on. LaKeya's parents and my parents made sure that she and I excelled in school. Getting C's on our report card was not an option, and B's were based on the subject if the subject was difficult. For example, I did not succeed in Science, so my parents allowed a B. By the time, LaKeya and I were in high school, most of the girls in our neighborhood were pregnant or just having their babies; we were no more than thirteen or fourteen years old. Our parents were destined to make sure that we did not end up in the ghetto. For me, I knew that I wanted to be a writer when I was young. I told my parents, and I was determined to write my way out of poverty from that moment. I was also determined not to be confined to anyone. I wanted and needed to work for myself.

I didn't want to be signed to some major publishing company. Yes, the perks were good. I would love to start out with a thirty thousand dollar advance and write. I could type away at my laptop until my fingers were numb. Go on book tours and meet exciting people. However, all that would be organized and structured by the major publishing company, and I didn't want that when they wanted me to want it. I wanted to go to exotic places, meet interesting people when I want to. I don't want to be signed to some kind of three or four-book deal and be forced to write something and produced a book on command. If I work for myself, I say when the book would be published. So I studied business, how to run, market, and promote my own business. I also studied the kings and queens on social media. I build my brand on social media, creating a business that social media pays me for posts and promos. I learned the art of self-publishing, how to market, sell and promote my book, and an independent author. Now, I make so much money that living on The Island is a dream now reality. I can buy what I want when I want.

LaKeya was primed to be a rich man's wife. From the way she dressed to how she acts in public. Lakeya dressed preppy, wore soft colors, pastels and pearls. She wears very little makeup, just enough mascara to make her pretty almond-shaped brown eyes pop and soft gloss that gives her lips a natural pout. She was always beautiful. With her soft brown eyes and pretty light-skinned, she had many admirers but she didn't date just anyone. She dated men that had prospects, going to a good college with a future in something secure. LaKeya didn't have talent. She couldn't sing her away out of the ghetto; she was born beautiful so she can marry rich. Her parents taught her to speak when spoken to. Never outshine her man, laugh at his jokes and never seem too eager.

Sometimes, LaKeya acts as if her past was some kind of myth, a funny fable that I enjoy telling. Sometimes she acts embarrassed when I relive the stories from the hood. I personally enjoy sharing my story because I am proud of where I came from especially considering where I am now, but LaKeya acts as if those days are forbidden secrets.

As I eat my shrimp that has been seasoned in garlic and lemon pepper served over flavor rice and sip my wine, I close my eyes and basks in the moment of the now, of the: Here I am.

"I think we should come every year," I said. "You know the boys run around."

"I guess," LaKeya said.

"What's your problem?" I ask. "You been pouty and weird all day."

"I'm fine." She said.

I know why she is pouty. I can see it; it's as clear as day. She is mad that I am famous, that I am more than what she thought of me to be. I eat away at my shrimp and sip my wine.

"When are you going to get married and have children?" she asks.

I scoff at the idea.

"I will get married when the right one comes along," I said.

"Do you think your boyfriend was intimidated by you?" she asks.

I shrug my shoulders.

"My boyfriend loved many women; that is why he is no longer my boyfriend," I said.

"Why, why did he cheat on you?" LaKeya asks.

"The same reason why dogs lick themselves." I said sarcastically. "Listen LaKeya, Marcus broke my heart. He made promises that he would not keep. He left me wondering if I wasn't enough. I questioned everything, was I not ladylike enough in society, was I not freaky enough in the bedroom, was I not Clever enough."

"Clever?" LaKeya asks.

"June Clever," I said, shaking my head. "Was I not the Bonnie to his Clyde? I brought him a car and helped with the first and last month's rent for his home. I was that girl, but he wanted other women!"

I watch LaKeya shake her head at what I said.

"Do you regret doing all that for him?" LaKeya asked.

I shake my head and then sipped my wine.

"No?" she asked.

"No," I answer.

"How can you not regret what you did for him? You paid for him to disrespect you."

"That is why I don't regret it! I chose to do all those things. I was letting him do those things. Was I hurt, of course, am I dead, no. I realized that I am not going to pay for you to disrespect me; I am no longer going to give you that opportunity. And so the week before I came here, he called, blowing up my phone, wanting who knows what. I packed my bags and came here."

"So you ran from him," LaKeya stated.

"I guess," I shrugged. " but in my defense, I am not obligated to him, so I didn't have to return his phone calls or give him any explanation to where I am."

"Obligated?"

"Booker is your husband," I said. "You better answer the phone when he calls."

She looks at her plate and eats her salad.

"Anyway, I am here. Not just on The Island, but I am here living my life, living my dream. I'm free."

"You're free because you are single?" LaKeya asks.

"No, I am free because I can do what I want. Come and go as I please. Key, you and I were not able to do this when we were kids. Our lives were consumed with shootings outsides, drug deals, girls we went to school with getting pregnant, absent fathers, and mentally unstable mothers. I am also free because I refused to be confined in a dead-end relationship. Being with Marcus left me stuck-mentally. I did not know if I was coming or going if he was my man, my friend, or someone he wanted for the evening. I have the power to come and go as I please. I tell you when I speak with you. I am away on a summer vacation; no one can dictate to me who I am or where I belong."

We sit in silence for a moment.

"I don't feel free," LaKeya said. "I am Mrs. Booker Matthews, and soon I will be the boys' mother. I have no identity."

I look at her.

"This is the life you wanted, Key," I said in a cool manner. "You wanted to be a rich man's wife."

"I wanted some kind of substance. You brought everything today, you. Me, Booker brought it, not me."

I look at her. I almost feel sorry for her, but it a strange and sadistic way; I am happy that she is seeing me. I am happy that she is not fulfilled.

"That dress, those shoes, exudes your beauty, making your dark skin stand out. Your hair is in the most unflattering hairstyle, but the way you wear it, it's worn like a crown."

I don't know if I should take her words as a compliment or is giving concede that I am not the ugly friend that she once thought of me to be.

"You're famous." She said, rolling her eyes. "Everyone here knows you and actually reads your work."

"So, my pretty friend, do something! Start a charity or start your own business. You have children now; get involved in the school PTA's."

There is a sudden shift in the air; a cool breeze began to flow. I can smell fresh flowers. I look at LaKeya. I realized that something has changed within her. Is a spark of interest in actually doing something else with her life instead of being a rich man's wife?

"I need to focus right now on the boys' christening." She said.

I watch her sit up and become this regal woman that has too much to do and not enough time.

"I need to confirm the pastor, the food, and the staff, also the guest list; I must see the florist."

LaKeya summons the waiter for the check.

"I will pick up the check," she said to me.

"Okay," I reply.

42

3

I SIT IN THE Great Room of the loft, watching mind-numbing television, thinking about the events from my morning. My best friend jealous of me from the way I look at my success. I slowly walk to the back of the Great Room. There is a glass door that leads to the balcony that overlooks the balcony. I see fireworks in the sky. There must be some kind of party or celebration. Apart of me wants to go and socialize, but I don't know anyone. LaKeya is focused on making the boys' christening some kind of grand celebration. I smile at the fact that today, I realized that I am some kind of celebrity, I don't necessarily need a buddy to party with, but it would be nice to build those memories—my cell phone rings. I rush to it, thinking it's one of my friends that I left behind when I left for The Island, asking me how my vacation is so far, but to my surprise, it is Marcus. I take in a deep breath. I don't bother to answer it. I hit ignore; I let the phone ring out.

Marcus Peterson, the one man whom I thought was going to be the one. I sigh at the thought and then shake my head. I loved him. We met at a party in New York. I was the famous writer, living out my Carrie Bradshaw fantasy. I was dressed fabulously in my LBD, and I wore royal blue Guess platform shoes. My dreadlocks were wavy from them being in a two-strained twist style. I had my three other girlfriends there, so that night was very *Sex in the City*. I was happy, living my dream. I laughed with my friends, interacted with other people, and networking. I saw him from across the room; he was handsome. He stood tall, dark-skinned with a goat-tee. His body was thick, like a football player; his shoulders were broad. From the moment I saw him, I liked him. I smiled at him as I interacted with my friends and associates. I noticed him smiling at me. My friends noticed him, and they smiled at me. As he walked towards me, I felt butterflies floating in my stomach.

"Hello," he said, smiling at me.

"Hi," I reply back.

"My name is Marcus, Marcus Peterson."

"I'm Journey Calloway," I said.

"I know who you are." He said.

I couldn't help but grin and shoot my friends a quick glance.

"I see you all over social media, and I have read some of your work."

I nodded my head.

"What do you do?" I asked.

"I am a fashion buyer." He answers.

I nodded my head. I saw a handsome man and free clothes. Immediately I thought he was the one. Throughout the evening, Marcus and I talked and flirted with each other. The following weekend, Marcus and I were on our first date. It seemed to be a romantic event. We had a candlelight dinner, and we walked under the stars. He told me that he would love to be the buyer for high-end fashion boutiques. His mother was a seamstress and one-time promising fashion designer and had a few of her clothing in the smaller boutiques. At the time, Marcus helped negotiate her deals and prices for the boutiques. His money management and business savvy skills made him well known within the fashion community, and many local and talented designers called upon him to get their fashion in boutiques. Fashion magazines wanted him to help style some of their campaigns.

Besides writing, there was nothing glamorous life about my life. However, the fact that I tour doing my speaking engagements or book signings seemed glamorous enough with him.

"Imagine the idea of getting dressed up and then having your picture in the paper," Marcus said, smiling.

"That is the fun part." I laughed.

For the few months, it was as if Marcus and I were inseparable. We spent almost every day and night together. We made passionate love and ate expensive foods, drank wine. However, I did notice that I did most of the buying. His money was tied up with this bank waiting on checks to clear or he was waiting on a boutique to sign on to a deal with a major designer for him to get his share of the profits. I didn't see the red flags at first because I saw his books, I saw his contracts, I saw his bank statements. So I believed that his money was tied up or he was waiting, plus as black woman, I wanted to support my black man. I wanted to be the one that he could count on and rely on. I saw a vision of us together, a type of power couple. We looked good at parties and events; people seemed to know him just like they knew me.

Then one morning, while sitting at home sipping on my morning latte and reading the paper. I saw him in the pictures smiling, looking happy with a beautiful woman on his arm. A pretty light-skinned beauty with long dark brown hair, she had hazel-colored eyes. She was very, very beautiful, the kind of woman that any man would be proud to have on his arm. At first, I wanted to believe that she was some kind of model, and he was sealing a deal with a designer, and they were smiling together, sharing a laugh, and the camera caught these beautiful people. However, I saw that he was holding her hand, their fingers interlocking.

I had no clue that there was some kind of event that evening. As a matter of fact, he told me that he had work to do and that he'll call me in the morning. After looking at the article and the picture, immediately, I called him.

"Hello," he answered the phone, sounding groggy.

I had awoken him up.

"Good morning," I said sternly.

"Hey," he said coolly.

"How was your evening?" I ask.

"It was fine; what's up?" he asks; I can tell he was stretching.

"I saw the picture in the paper! Who is that woman?" I asked.

"What picture? What paper!" he asks.

"What picture? What paper?" I ask. "*The Times*, there is a picture of you and some woman! Who is that woman? Why didn't you tell me about the event?"

"She is nothing!" Marcus said coolly. "Just a model at the event, an old friend. Baby, let's grab a bite to eat."

I shook my head at how easy he was able to pass off the woman and the event.

"Why didn't you tell me about the event?"

"Because it was nothing, nothing major, nothing big. I just went for the free food and free drinks?"

Free food and free drinks. That statement rings in my head as I look back. He had been dating me for the month that is all he had, free food and free drinks. I paid for everything. He could have had free drinks and free food with me that night. Marcus came to my house later that morning. He brought me a dozen of orange roses and a tennis bracelet.

"Listen, baby, I'm sorry." He said. "I should have said something, but the truth is. I just wanted to go out and do me."

"Do you?" I asked.

"Yes, baby, it's been you and me. I just wanted to do me, alone."

Marcus set the roses down, and he stepped closer to me and kissed me, passionately igniting forgiveness. From that moment on, it seemed like a tug of war trying to get him to see me. I saw and heard of him going out on the town with beautiful and famous women. Most of the places he went to were for fashion-related events, so I convinced myself that he was working, he was networking, but I knew the truth, he was dating other women, but coming home to me after he was too tired to do anything or go anywhere. I justified that the fact that I had him eventually was okay, that he is spending his evenings with me. I would lie next to him in bed, caressing him. I was pretending that during that time, it was our intimate time. As we laid under the covers, close to each other, we looked into each other eyes and discussing our dreams. I savored each moment because I didn't know when I would see him again. I didn't know *if* I would see him again.

Any negative energy I felt whenever he was not with me, I put in my work, I wrote more, booked more speaking events, but I was unhappy. I wanted Marcus with me when I would tour, to see me working to see me networking. I did everything I could for him to want to be loyal to me. If I paid his bills, he would appreciate me and see that I was the woman that was holding him down. If I paid for some of his business needs, then he would see that I had his back, but the more I gave, the more it gave him that window to do what he wanted, using the excuse that he was working and that he was networking and it would be a matter of time that he and I would get married and really live the dream together.

Then one day, I was watching television. Marcus was on television discussing his business, and he was not alone. There was a beautiful woman, like the pretty woman in the newspaper picture I saw. She was light skinned, long hair, pretty hazel colored eyes. Marcus introduced her as his fiancé. My stomach dropped. I never felt more alone in my life. Immediately my phone rang. It was my friends calling to see if I was watching the television.

"Yes, I'm watching it," I said.

I was too numb to cry.

"I don't have anything to say,' I said to my friends on the phone.

The truth was, I literally had nothing to say. There was no justifying his actions. He wasn't working or networking business deals with models and designers. He was simply using me to get whatever he needed. He needed the nice apartment that I paid first and last month's rent for to entertain his lady friends. How ironic that I did not notice that I never had a key to that apartment. He needed money for business cards and his marketing to get into those parties to meet new women. Marcus would tell me it would be for networking, but it would be for simple socializing.

After seeing Marcus on television with his fiancé, I didn't bother to call him. My girlfriends came to my home, and we ate and drank Moscato and bashed men.

"I blame myself," I said, drinking my wine.

"No, no, girl!" my friends said. "He was a dog!"

I shake my head.

"He was a bad man, but I allowed him to be a bad man! I knew better! I knew that he was stepping out on me. He was bold enough to do so openly, and I was stupid enough to believe his lie or try to justify his lie."

I allowed the sex to fog my thinking. The sex was better than good. His smile was charming; I shook my head at his charm because as much as I knew that he was full of nonsense, I wanted to believe that maybe just maybe, he was telling me his truth. I noticed that the woman that Marcus was engaged to was light-skinned; she is beautiful, compared to my dark-skin. She had pretty long hair, which is far from my natural course hair that is worn in dreadlocks. I was too dark for him, too urban, not conservative enough.

I looked at my friends; there were three of them, all brown-skinned beauties and different individuals. One woman, Candice, similar to LaKeya, is a conservative beauty. She wore her hair in a short pixie cut and pearl earrings. There is Tameka; she wore her hair natural, sometimes, her hair would be worn wild and in an Afro style or in an Afro puff. There is Racquel; she had long hair that she got relaxed every few months, a woman of sophistication. These three ladies looked like me, dark-skinned, but they were proud of who they are and what they have accomplished. Only Racquel and I worked for ourselves. Tameka worked in retail, and Candice worked for an insurance company as a manager.

"I was too black for him," I said.

My friends shook their heads at my comment because there is a strong possibility that it was true. Marcus' fiancé was light-skinned and thin-framed. I am dark-skinned with curves.

The next day, LaKeya called to tell me about the twins and about the christening. I was beyond happy for her!

"You have to come; we will be vacationing on The Island. You can stay with Booker and me."

"No, no," I said, smiling. "With the new babies, I can find a place to rent for the summer."

I knew the reputation of The Island. Rich African-Americans living the dream, drinking tea and sitting at the country club. I knew about the old money and new money. With The Island being so far away, it was perfect timing to get out of the city and away from my emotional scandal.

MY CELL PHONE RINGS, distracting me from my thoughts. I look to see who is calling. I pray that it is Marcus for the satisfaction that he is calling, and I also pray that it is not because as much as I don't want to talk with him, I do want to talk with him. However, when I look at the phone, I see that it is an unrecognized number. I am nervous because maybe Marcus is calling me from someone's phone number. Intrigued, I answer the phone.

"Hello," I said sternly.

"Journey, hi, it's Nathan." Said the voice on the phone.

"Hey, Nathan," I said. "How did you get my number?"

"LaKeya," he answered quickly.

I rolled my eyes. She knows that I don't like her giving out my phone number to anyone. I shake my head, but after the goofy way she has been talking to me today, maybe something is wrong.

"What's up? Is everything all right?" I asked.

"Yeah, yeah," Nathan answers. "I was just wondering would you like to go to a party tonight. I hear Vision Campbell is throwing one of her many parties. They are life! From live music, food, alcohol, entertainment."

"Entertainment?! Is that what these fireworks are for?"

"Yes, Vision Campbell does it big!" Nathan said.

I wanted to see this Vision Campbell.

"Okay!" I said. "I can meet you there!"

"No, no, I'll come get you," Nathan said. "LaKeya said you're staying in her loft. I can be there in an hour."

"Okay."

A party thrown by Vision Campbell; I run into the bedroom and go through my clothes. What does one wear to a party hosted by Vision Campbell? As I tear in through the closet tossing clothes around that I have yet to hang up, I search frantically for something elegant, chic, and stylish to wear. What does she look like? I want to look her in the eyes and formally shake her hand and say,

"I'm the one renting your loft! Your loft is beautiful! Can I secure it for next year?"

I find an outfit. A sleeveless, black silk jumpsuit with a metallic gold and silver belt. Quickly I shower, and I stand in my bath towel in front of the mirror; I try to figure out how to do my dreadlocks. I pull them up, styling my locks into a high bun. I put on a pair of silver and black hood earrings. I do my make-up, a natural look with a pop of red lips. I hear the doorbell ring. I look at the clock; Nathan is ten minutes early. This isn't a date, so it really doesn't matter how I look just yet; I am dressing to meet Vision Campbell.

I run to the door, and without looking out of the window, I open the door. Nathan is standing before me. He smiles at me.

"Hi," he said, smiling. "You look good."

"Thank you, come in."

I step aside so Nathan can enter inside. I shut the door.

"I need to get finish getting ready. Can I get you anything to drink or eat?"

"No, I'm okay."

I nod my head and lead him in the Great Room.

"Okay, well, please have a seat, make yourself comfortable."

"Thanks," Nathan said.

Quickly I walked back to the bedroom to finish primping. I look in the mirror to make sure I look perfect. I want to look perfect for Vision Campbell. When she meets me, I want to be perfect for her.

"You're renting the loft," I can hear her say.

"Yes, a beautiful home!" I would say.

"Well, thank you."

We would take selfies together, and I would put them on social media, my Instagram, my Facebook page, and we would Snapchat. I would get so many likes and comments.

I take in a deep breath, slide into my black high heel platforms, and grab my black clutch. Quickly I return to Nathan. He has taken the remote control and changed the channel to some ESPN.

He stands as he sees me. I smile. Nathan takes the remote and turns the television off. He approaches me, smiling.

"You look real good." He said.

"Thanks," I said.

I finally look at him; he looks nice. He wears a silk maroon-colored button-up and black slacks. He wears black leather shoes. Together we leave the loft; as I lock the door, I hear him click the button on his key chain to unlock the door. Nathan walks me to the passage side of the car and opens the door for me.

"Thanks," I said.

He grins, and as I get in the car and put my seat belt on, I see him walk around the car to get into his side. Once inside, he puts his seat belt on and starts the car, and we race off.

"Have you ever been to Vision Campbell's party?" I ask.

He nods.

"What are they like?"

"Like a Diddy party." He jokes. "Live."

"Oh man," I said, smiling. "I am very excited. Have you ever met Vision Campbell?"

Nathan nods his head.

"Really?" I asks. "What is she like?"

"She is quiet." Nathan answers. "She likes to watch people celebrate. She is very giving."

"You know I am renting her loft," I said proudly.

"I know," Nathan said. "You act as if you never met her?"

"I haven't."

"You didn't meet her when you rented the loft?" Nathan asked.

"No, she had one of her minions meet me to sign the lease," I answered.

"You seen her," Nathan said.

I shook my head.

"She is a model," Nathan said.

"I know, but I never saw her."

Nathan pointed to a picture of a woman on the billboard. As the car drives up towards the billboard and drives away, I see the picture of the beautiful woman. She is light-skinned, with hazel-colored eyes, and she wears her auburn-colored hair in dreadlocks. I gasp.

"That is her?!" I exclaimed.

"Yes," Nathan laughs at me. "You never knew that is Vision Campbell?"

"No!"

Then my mind reflects to the airplane and the sign that was in the air last night white at Booker and LaKeya's; it was an image of Vision Campbell.

"She was on that picture that was floating across the sky while at Keys and Book's. She is the woman you were talking about!"

"Yeah," Nathan said.

We pull up to a red light.

"So she is trying to get Booker back?" I ask.

"I don't know if she is trying to get him back, but she is trying to get his attention."

"Why?" I ask.

"What do you mean why? You know how you women are." Nathan chuckled.

"Men do it too," I said, folding my arms across my chest.

"Whatever." Nathan laughed. "Anyway, she throws parties every weekend. Big parties, with live music, live entertainment."

I nod my head. I am excited. I am going to meet Vision Campbell. Just being on The Island, I heard about her elusive demeanor. Christina and her staff seemed to hesitate to discuss her. I look at Nathan.

"When LaKeya and I went to Christina's this afternoon, the staff seemed distant when I mentioned Vision Campbell. Is it because of Key?"

"No, Vision and Booker were together long before she was famous." Nathan answers.

"So why were they so distant?" I asked.

"I don't know Journey," Nathan said, chuckled. "Why are you so obsessed with Vision?"

"Why not?" I exclaim. "She is a mystery. Like, I am staying in her loft, and it has been decorated *so* nice. Plus, she sent one of her assistance to give me the keys to the loft, so it's like, why didn't *she* come."

"Because she is Vision Campbell, she doesn't have to show up," Nathan replied.

"I get that, but she seems reclusive; why?"

Nathan drives the car to a gate.

"We're here." He said.

I smile. I see a crowd of people

Nathan gets out of the car, and I quickly get out. He walks around the car to me.

"I was going to open the door for you." He said.

"Oh," I said, feeling embarrassed. "I'm sorry."

Nathan takes my hand and leads me to the front entrance. The house is like Booker and LaKeya's mansion. The mansion is a large 23,000 square foot house. There is a crowd of people, an enormous amount of people congregating in the front of the courtyard trying to get into the mansion. This makes me think of an exclusive club only certain people can get in. As the people socialize and mingle with each other, they danced to the live music that was blasting from the speakers. Nathan grabs my hand, I assume, so we don't lose each other in the sea of people. As Nathan leads me to the front, I look in the crowd hoping to see Vision. I don't see her. Nathan walks to the front door standing is a butler and a bouncer. Both men standing; one with their arms folded across their chest and the other with their chest out and their hands at their sides.

"Nathan Moore and Journey Calloway," Nathan informs.

Both men nod their heads and step aside allowing, Nathan and I to enter. Like outside, a crowd of people, standing in the foyer, mingled and talked among themselves. As we walk through the crowd, I notice the photos of Vision Campbell. Some of the photos are black in white, some color, and she is radiant and beautiful. I see photos of her with famous politicians. As we continue to walk through the house, the more people I see. They are dancing to the loud music. The butlers are serving drinks, from Champaign to white wine, red wine. They serve different types of hors d'oeuvre, shrimp cocktail, stuffed mushrooms, salmon bites, steak, and mushroom bites, on the trays.

"Do you want something to drink?" Nathan asks.

I shake my head.

56

I continue to search the room and the sea of people for Vision Campbell. I don't see her here.

"Nate, Nate!" someone calls out.

Nathan and I both look to see who is calling us. It is a male, a brown-skinned man. He has a wide smile as he approaches us.

"Hey, Victor!" Nathan said. "This is my friend, Journey Calloway."

"The writer?" Victor asks, shaking my hand.

"Yes," I answer with a smile.

"Victor Williams is a stockbroker," Nathan informed.

I grinned.

"Some party," Victor said, shaking his head.

"Yeah," Nathan said.

"She throws these parties every week." Victory said to me.

I nod my head, indicating I know.

"What are these parties for?" I ask.

"For The New," Nathan said.

"The New?" I ask.

"Yes,"

"You mean for The New Money?" I ask.

"Yep," Victor said.

"She throws a party for new money?" I ask again. "Why?"

"Because The Established don't like us," Victor said. "They don't think we earned our rights. So Vision throws parties every weekend to show The Established that we earned our place in society. It's a more, in your face type of thing."

I look at Nathan.

"That is kind of petty," I said.

"It's Vision Campbell," Victor said with a chuckle. "Well, I see a pretty thing that I need to dance with. Nate, call me tomorrow, we can do lunch."

"Yep," Nathan replies.

We watch Victor leave. Nathan looks at me.

"Let's dance," Nathan said.

He takes me by the hand and leads me to an empty spot on the dance floor. The band is live. The singer is a beautiful, brown-skinned beauty with long jet black hair. She is singing a fast tempo song. Her band members play trumpets, keyboards, drums, bass guitars. Her name or the band name must begin with the letter A because there are large blocks on the stage with the letter A on them. She is rocking; she wears black bikini bottoms with black fishnet stocking and five-inch high heel shoes. She wears a black and red suit jacket. As I dance with Nathan, I watch her dance, swinging her hips and moving her legs with the beat of the music.

I look at Nathan; he is smiling at me. I sway my body back and forth to the beat. I put my arms around Nathan's shoulders and begin to dance harder, enjoying the music. However, I think about what Victor said. This party is for The New. Why waste time proving a point to people that don't care, The Established. I realize that I had to prove myself to LaKeya. Prove to her that I am more than some kind of internet sensation. The money that she came into is by marriage, which is old money. I can think or act as if she, too, is The New. Because who is to say that her marriage will last. Booker can get tired of her and divorce her. I don't want to think like that; I want to think that She and Booker will live happily ever after, with their beautiful boys and more children.

"Hey," Nathan said.

We continue to dance. I look at him. He is smiling at me a smile that tells me that he likes me. I smile back and continue to dance.

NATHAN AND I STAND on the balcony. The air is surprisingly cool, considering how humid The Island is. I hold on to the rail and lean back, tilting my head back. Music still plays, I sway with the beat with hopes that I can encourage the cool air to engulf me.

"You having fun?"

Nathan asks as a butler comes with a tray of Champaign. I watch Nathan take two glasses off the tray and gives me a glass. I sip the drink.

"This is nice," I said, shaking my head.

"What's nice?" he asks, sipping his drink.

"This home, this atmosphere," I answer. "She is a model. All this on a models' salary?"

"No, Vision has her money in other projects," Nathan said, walking towards me.

"So what happened with her and Booker?" I ask.

Nathan grin.

"Why?" he asks.

"Just curious," I reply. "All this to prove to the world that you're special."

"Who cares? It's free booze and shrimp, every Nigga's dream." Nathan jokes.

I laugh.

"Serious, Journey," Nathan said. "Are you always so deep?"

I take in a deep breath and then sip the Champaign.

"Yes, I am a thinker. I'm a writer." I said.

"You're an over-thinker." Nathan said. "LaKeya told me about you."

"About me?" I ask.

"Yeah, she told me you analysis and think about everything." He said. "Relax, you are on vacation in one of the most beautiful places in the world. You are renting a loft from the world's most beautiful woman; you are partying at her home and looking very good."

Nathan set's his glass down on the small stand in the corner of the balcony and slowly approaches me. He stands beside me, looking down at me. I quickly look up at him, hoping that I don't see what I think I see, but I do. I see a handsome man looking at me, hoping that I will indulge in his coy advances. The cool breeze allows me to smell his cologne, the musk cologne that ignites a spark in me.

"I also asked LaKeya if you have a man." He said.

I nod my head and focus my attention on the dark shadow that, after squinting hard enough, I determined it is a tree.

"I think you kind of fly." He said.

I chuckle at his line.

"I know my line is corny, but-," Nathan stops talking. "You build your business on the backbone of the hustle. No bank loans, no credit loans, no friend loans, just flipped your money and hustled."

"Thank you," I said.

"That is how The New was made," Nathan said.

"Excuse me?" he asks.

"The New. They had little to nothing, took their dollar and flipped it, and kept flipping until they own the blocks, community, the city, and so forth. They were determined to live the dream instead of being someone else's."

60

I grinned at the thought. I am living my dream. I am not working for no one. I don't report to a supervisor or manager. I don't have to punch in or punch out.

"How did you get your money?" I ask. "I mean-,"

"I know what you mean," Nathan answered. "I'm a sports agent. These knuckle-headed ballplayers, I warned about their money. I warned them that white man don't care about you. Your job is to get on the field, play your game and go home. I said to them that if they're good, endorsements will come, but speak when spoken to, refrain from negative comments because that will cost you money."

"What if you get some rogue?" I asked.

"They have to find a new agent. I don't represent foolishness." Nathan said. "Anyway, Journey, I am not here to talk The New or The Established. I'm here to talk to you."

I let out a sign.

"I'm not dating right now," I answered. "I'm doing me."

I look at Nathan, wondering if I can say those words to a handsome man and mean it, but as I said them and looked at this handsome man, not only do I not mean them, but I don't believe them.

"What are you doing?" Nathan asked.

"Me," I answer. "You know, focusing on me,"

"What else is there to focus on? You are successful, rich, and beautiful." Nathan said. "Listen, we are on a reclusive island for the summer. Let's have fun, get drunk, and forget about The New and The Establish and be do us."

The idea sounds tempting. I look at Nathan, I grinned. The singer started to sing a slow song. Nathan gently grabs me by the waist and moves me close to him and we begin to slow dance. I look up at him. His eyes are gentle and trusting. I can feel my body temperature rising, I don't know if it's the scenery, the heat or my lonely heart, but I am feeling vulnerable in his arms. I want to be held and I want to be looked at the way Nathan is looking at me right now. I let out a sigh. Nathan lean and kisses me. His lips are soft, soft enough for me to indulge in his kiss and kiss him back, harder and passionately.

I pull back and let out a sigh catching my breath. I shake my head.

"We can't, we can't" I said, pushing away from Nathan's hold.

"Why not?" Nathan reaches for me.

"Because, we are godparents. LaKeya's babies' godparents." I shake my head.

"Journey, we are not related." He chuckled.

I WAKE UP TO see Nathan standing at the window, looking at the scenery.

I sit up. Nathan turns around to see me. I smile at him. He smiles back. He is fully dressed. I look down at myself, the covers covering me, but I know that I am naked under the covers. Our night was intense yet passionate. We left Vision Campbell's party and came back to the loft. Nathan walked me to the door, and as I unlocked the door, we were passionately kissing, pushing our way into the loft. I shut and locked the door and returned to his lips. Nathan lifted me up in his arms. We walk into the bedroom, and together we fell upon the bed. We continue to kiss each other passionately. My body was on fire, and I needed Nathan to put the fire out. He made me feel good; he made me feel beautiful; he made me feel wanted. However, I don't want to get too caught up in my feelings or desires. I don't want to get hurt again, plus this is a fling.

As I sit up in the bed looking at him, I am surprised that he stayed.

"You're still here," I said.

"Yeah," Nathan said. "Want to do something today?" he asked.

"Sure," I answered. "Wait, no. LaKeya wants us at the estate to go over the christening rehearsal."

Nathan shakes his head.

"She acts as if this is some kind of wedding," I state.

"Yes, all of the big names and big money will be there. Potential banking privilege for Booker. LaKeya host a grand christening that means more money for Booker."

I nod my head. I take in a deep breath.

"I'm going to freshen up," I said.

I turn to the edge of the bed and grab my robe and slide it on. I walk into the bathrobe and walk into the bathroom. I shut the door and lean against the door and let out a sigh, my body still tingling from the night before. I don't know if I am still horny or was Nathan that good. I wash my face, brush my teeth and return to the bedroom. Nathan is not there, but he's in the kitchen. I hear him moving pots and pans around. I walk into the kitchen.

"You cook?" I asked.

Nathan turns to face me with a grin.

"Sit down." He says.

I sit down, and Nathan places a cup of coffee in front of me. I grin at him. Nathan sits down in the chair next to me.

"Last night was good," I say.

"Last night was real good," Nathan said.

He takes my hands into his. I look at him. I'm nervous. I know those taking my hands in to his moves. I take in a deep breath. I don't want to be the one who is dump or told: *Let's be friends.*

"Nathan, you don't owe me anything." I blurted out.

"What do you mean?" he asked.

"I mean, we just met, we're on vacation, and we're here for a christening. So-,"

"I told you last night; I want to ya know spend time with you while we are here on The Island." He said.

"Like a couple, until it's time to go our separate ways," I ask rhetorically.

Nathan shrugs.

"That sounds kind of strange, but I am thinking, let's have fun, enjoy our summer and see where this goes."

I take in a deep breath and nod my head. I think I can handle this type of relationship. It's a no-strings policy. I don't have to get caught up and hope that we're that Will and Jada power couple. I have a friend, spend some time with, go to the movies or the theater with. We can eat Chinese food in bed and cold pizza in bed. We can christen our godsons and sunbathe on the beach. While he fixes breakfast, I can sit on the patio and brainstorm. After the summer, I can go back to my house in New York, think fondly of our time, and for the first time smile. Because I did not set myself up to get hurt, and if we happen to see each other next year at the boys' first birthday because I know that LaKeya will have a grand celebration, I will see Nathan and hope that he comes solo. After the birthday party, we sneak off to each other's hotel suite and reminisce on our time on The Island, and under the covers create the passionate magic that we shared and will share.

"Journey," Nathan says, calling me from my thoughts.

"Yes," I said.

"I'm not asking for a commitment, just hoping for a little summer fun," Nathan said.

I grinned.

"Why not," I said, smiling.

I sip my coffee, and Nathan leans in to kiss me, and I determined that I am that horny and he was that good.

4

I WAS SOMEWHAT APPREHENSIVE about arriving at LaKeya and Booker's mansion with Nathan. I don't know why I am nervous about LaKeya and Booker finding out about Nathan and me. However, when we arrived, several of Booker and LaKeya's rich friends were already at the mansion, so no one noticed. As LaKeya focused on the seating chart for the dining hall, everyone sipped on mimosa's and eat seafood salad or steak.

"Booker, I still need a confirmation on Philip and Stephanie Golden," LaKeya said.

"Who are they?" I ask.

"Only the richest lawyers in California." LaKeya answers. "We can use their investments in the bank."

I nod my head. I walk to LaKeya and see her working on the seating chart. It's a large poster board with several circles, the circles indicating tables. On the circles were several tabs, all different colors, and on the tabs are names.

"LaKeya, what are these?" I ask.

"The green tabs are for the investors, businessmen and women and entrepreneurs. The blue tabs are for celebrities, the yellow tabs are for socialites, the black tabs are for lawyers, judges, and politicians, and the white tabs are for the family. Speaking of, Booker my parents said they would be here by the weekend."

"Miss Donna and Mr. Jake are coming!" I exclaim, referring to LaKey's parents.

"Don't remind me," LaKeya said, rolling her eyes.

I chuckle.

"Your parents are wonderful," I said.

I look to their guest and friends.

"Have you met Key's parents?" I ask.

"Yes," they said variously.

I smile.

"Refined ghetto is always charming." One of their guests, named Monica, said.

"Excuse me?" I questioned.

Monica chuckles at her comment. The way she smirks, it is evident that she had Botox done. I shake my head at her because she looks plastic and fake. She is light-skinned, with a thin nose. She looks like a lost member of the Jackson Family; her thin lips are heavy coated with gloss. She wears blue contact leans in her eyes It is evident that they are bothering her because throughout the afternoon she has been squinting or winking at everyone and wearing a blond wing. I look at her fingers; large cubic Zirconium stones are on her fingers, her manicure is French acrylic manicure. She sits in the seat wearing a soft yellow dress with her cleavage exposed. The dress is so short that whenever she sits, she has to sit with a pillow on her lap.

"Journey, you're going to learn that some people just don't belong in our world," Monica said to me, holding her mimosa.

"What world is that?" I asked.

"You have the people that were born poor and worked their way to the top, like the Obamas, Oprah, and you have those that just want to be on top, like LaKeya's parents."

I look at LaKeya. I am shocked that she is allowing this woman to speak badly of her parents.

"If it wasn't for Key's parents' sacrifice, Key wouldn't be here, serving you the mimosa."

Monica rolls her eyes at me.

"They were born to raise LaKeya into the refined and beautiful young lady that she is today. She is obligated to bring them along. Everyone can't come where you are."

I take in a deep breath. I shake my head at Monica's statement. I look at Booker; he grins and then shrugs his shoulders. I look at LaKeya, hoping and waiting for a defense."

"Journey, my world is too refined for my parents. It's like a bull in a glass shop. I love them of course. I would do anything for them, but my world is diamond, pearls, and silk. They are cheap polyester and costume jewelry from Walmart."

"What do your parents do, *Journey*?" Monica asks, stressing my name.

"My father made pipes, and my mother was a secretary for a pharmaceutical company," I said proudly. "Now they are retired, and they travel."

"How nice," she said, twisting her lips.

"Why are they not here, on The Island?" she asks, hoping to prove a point.

"Because my vacation conflicted with their travels plans to Dubai," I answer with a smirk.

Monica looks at me, wanting to say something degrading about my parents.

"Ladies!" Booker quickly intervened.

I step back and take in a deep breath. I look at LaKeya and shake my head, and quickly I walk out to the back yard that leads to the garden. I hear footsteps behind me; it's Nathan. I lean my head back and let out a sigh.

"That woman is-,"

"I know, I know." He says to me. "Don't let that get to you."

"Get to me? She basically called me and LaKeya's parents trash! Look at her; that is Ghetto Fabulous!"

"Listen, she's a wanna be, seriously Journey, she is not worth it," Nathan said.

"What happened with LaKeya?" I ask. "She was always a little stuck up, but seriously what happened?"

"She needs to fit into Booker's world. The high society does not take kindly to urban culture." Nathan said.

"Then why am I here?" I ask. "Why am I here as her children's Godmother? I am just as urban and-,"

"You have more class than any of those women in that sitting room," Nathan said to me.

I am too annoyed with LaKeya and her friend that I missed his compliment.

"Journey!" I hear my name called. "Journey!"

Nathan and I turn around and see LaKeya approaching us.

"Nate, can you leave Journey and me alone?" LaKeya request.

"Sure,"

I watch as Nathan walks away, leaving LaKeya and me alone. I look at her. She is pretty under the high sun, wearing a soft blue sundress with a spaghetti dress.

"What was that?" she asks.

"What was what?" I ask.

"You and Monica."

"Me and Monica?" I ask.

"Yes, why were you so rude to my friends?" LaKeya asks.

"Your friends were disrespecting your parents. Who would defend the very people who raised you, took care of you, and put you through college? Not you!"

"My parents don't need defending." LaKeya snap.

"No, but you don't let people disrespect your parents, your husband, or your children. That thing in there was blatantly disrespecting your family because they are not as rich as you? How can you with good conscious allow that?"

"Because it is. I don't want my parents to embarrass me at my children's christening." LaKeya said. "I have very important people coming, and the last thing Booker and I need are a bunch of ghetto niggas, ruining that."

"What has being in Booker's world done to you," I ask. "You were never this-,"

I am at a loss for words.

"Booker's World?" LaKeya asks. "Booker's World?"

"LaKeya, I'm not going to go tit for tat with you. I am not going to argue with you. If you want to shame your parents, go right ahead. Just know that I know you! I knew you when and this you is not the real you!"

I walk away, heading back inside. I hear LaKeya running behind me.

"Let me explain one thing to you." She said to me. "You will never succeed! Write your stupid books and live your life on social media as if you are some of star! I will always be prettier than you, richer than you, and better than you."

I look at her. I don't recognize her. I take in a deep breath and walk inside. I see Monica drinking more mimosa, Booker, Nathan, and a few other friends of theirs.

"Nathan, may I ask you for a ride home?" I said.

"Go!" LaKeya snaps.

Immediately Booker approaches LaKeya and holds her back.

"What is going on?" Booker asks.

"You will not be my son's godparents. They don't need you!"

"LaKeya!" Booker admonishes. "Joun-,"

"It's okay, Booker," I said. "Nate,"

"Let's go," Nathan said.

I follow Nathan out of the sitting room, down the long hallway that leads to the long foyer. I hold back tears, and we walk to Nathan's car. Nathan opens the door for me. I get inside, and then he gets in and quickly drives off. I want to scream; I want to cry. I want to go back in that mansion, grab LaKeya and shake the hell out of her. That is not my friend. That is some woman that possessed her body, making her mean and cold.

"Where do you want to go?" Nathan asks.

"You can take me back to the loft," I answer.

I DID NOT EXPECT him to want to stay with me, but I find myself sitting in the back yard of the loft sipping on ice water and lemon with Nathan sitting across from me. I didn't speak for a long time. I think about LaKeya, about our friendship. I think about growing up together, in the same housing projects. We took care of each other. When her parents worked late, she came to my house. My parents babysat her, I kept her company. She and I were never apart. I think about our dreams and goals. She used to encourage my writing. I would sit and read to her my stories; Key would listen inventively. LaKeya told me she dreams of being married to a rich man, so she can take care of her parents.

"They will never have to work again." LaKeya used to tell me.

"Mine too," I said.

She was always the girly girl. She always wore her pinks and soft girly colors, always had her hair in a pretty classic girl style. I will admit I was jealous, not in a hatred short of way, but a way that said, if I had her figure or her body. I was not shape like LaKeya. She had always had a figure to die for. She was petite and thin, me, I had more of a curvy figure. Thanks to Jennifer Lopez, Beyonce, and the Kardashian, curves are beautiful, so many people buy curves, butts, and thighs. Now that I am older, I have embraced my body, and I thank God for my body. I have embraced my dark skin and my nappy hair that is now in the form of dreadlocks.

As I sit on this patio, soaking in the sun, not caring that I get darker, I wonder if LaKeya was ever my friend. Growing up and going to school together, did I overlook her condescending comments about me? I don't remember her being mean to me. I remember her popularity increased in high school. She was beautiful and intelligent. The high school boys chased her, but she didn't consider any of them; they did not seem promising enough. She dated the boys whose fathers were lawyers or the boys that we on the debate teams or class president, and their parents had some kind of social ranking in society. Her quest for marrying a

72

rich man is or was nothing foreign to me. I knew that she wanted to be a kept woman. I remember hearing Miss Donna mention how she hopes that one day, LaKeya would marry up, that she would marry someone that would take good care of her. I remember how Mr. Jake, LaKeya's father warned her to never marry a man that cannot take care of her. If she choices not to work, she didn't have to. Mr. Jake raised LaKeya like a princess. I know that he worked hard to take care of her and Miss Donna. I know that every penny went to making his family happy. It bothered him that Miss Donna had to work. I know that she didn't mind, but they didn't want LaKeya to live like them.

As for me, my parents raised me to follow my dreams. It bothered me to see them go to a job, punch in and out, work on holidays and weekends, working for someone else. I know my parents had the talent to own their own business, but fear and economics hindered any dreams they had, but they encouraged me to go for my dreams. Although my writing is a gift, I went to writing school for two summers. I studied creative writing, and in college, I studied business. I knew that for me to be successful as an independent author, I need to learn how to run a business and marketing.

I hoped that once LaKeya and I graduated from college, we live the dream together. Of course, naturally, I knew that we would go our separate ways and have our separate lives, but her actions so far have been questionable. I want to call my mother and tell her, but I am too old to run home and call my mommy. I look at Nathan and smile.

"You didn't have to stay," I said to him.
"It's cool." Nathan said.

"You spent more time with them, is Booker doing something to her?" I ask.

"Booker is being Booker," Nathan said.

I nod my head, hoping that I get that answer, but I don't.

"What does that mean? Is Booker being Booker? The LaKeya I grew up with was not mean, nasty and condescending. We would not have had that woman Monica near her!"

"Monica is there so LaKeya can feel better about herself," Nathan said, drinking a beer.

"That is not Keya. She doesn't keep people around for her ego." I said.

Nathan sips his beer and shrugs his shoulders. I let out a sigh.

"Tell me how Booker was with Vision Campbell," I requested.

"What?" Nathan asks. "Listen, Journ; Vision Campbell just was not good enough for Booker, then."

"Why not?" I asked. "What makes someone not good enough?"

"First of all, look at her. She is the most beautiful woman in the world. Two, she was married and divorced. To Booker's family, that's a no-no, so they made him dump her."

I shake my head.

"What kind of family did she come from?" I asked.

"What does that have anything to do with anything?"

"Because the Matthews family expect someone to be refined and come from a good family. LaKeya's family, as you clearly learned do not come from the upper class, and he married Key. So what about Vision's family."

"I don't know about Vision's family. And considering that LaKeya keeps her family away, the Matthews don't say too much about LaKeya's family."

Nathan's answer is not enough for me, but I can tell that he doesn't want to talk about Vision Campbell, LaKeya, or Booker.

"I'm sorry, Nathan." I shake my head.

"You good, baby." He said to me with a grin. "Look, real talk, LaKeya is not happy. One would think that she is a rich husband, cute kids, living a life like a queen, but she is not happy. She sees you, a rich, independent woman; you're free."

"Free?" I ask.

"Yes, free," Nathan said. "Most married women want to be single; single women want to be married. You can come and go as you please. You are renting this loft, which I know for a fact it's a lot of money. You didn't stay with Booker and LaKeya's because you didn't have to. You were her friend from back in the day. She was promised the rich and privileged life; you were promised the sweet life of a go-getter."

"So I lose my friend because I have money?" I asked.

"You lose your friend because she's an idiot," Nathan said with a chuckle.

I let out a sigh. He stands up.

"Come on," he said, holding out his hand. "Let's put on some pastels, go to the country club, and fellowship with The Established."

"Why would I?" I answer, taking his hand.

"Because you paid a lot of money to hang out on The Island. Let's go hiking, swimming, shopping. Let's go!"

I smile at Nathan. He leans forward and kisses me. I smile at him.

"I appreciate you spending time with me during this issue," I said to Nathan.

He nods his head as he wraps his arms around me.

"Listen, you and LaKeya have been friends for years. You two will work this out. Will it be tomorrow, maybe not, but you will."

NATHAN AND I ENTER The Island Club. I smile at those that stop to take notice of us. One of the hostesses approaches us smiling. Nathan and I enter the country club, looking very much like a couple. We both wear pastel colors, me in a white tennis skirt, a mint green tank top with white tennis shoes, and a matching white sun visor. Nathan is wearing a mint green polo shirt and a pair of khaki shorts.

"Hi, Nathan,"

"Hey Veronica, allow me to introduce to you Journey Calloway,"

Veronica shakes my hand.

"I am a fan of your work." She says, smiling.

"Thank you," I answer.

"Nate!" we hear someone call out.

Nathan and I turn around to see Victor smiling at us.

"Hey, Vic," Nathan said, smiling. "You remember Journey Calloway."

"Oh yes," Victor said, smiling. "You two want to golf?"

"Yes," Nathan said, smiling.

"Mya and Ricky are outside waiting to tee off," Victor informed.

"Oh, okay, good," Nathan said, then looks at me. "You'll love Mya and Ricky."

Together the three of us walk onto the golf course and see whom I am to assume is Mya and Ricky. They smile as Nathan, Victor, and I approach them.

"Nathan!" Mya exclaims, with her arms open.

Nathan embraces her with a hug and kiss on the cheek. Then he smiles and shakes Ricky's hand.

"I was hoping to see you on The Island this summer," Ricky said.

"I'm here; I'm here. You know Booker just had his twins, and they are doing this very big christening." Nathan informed.

"Anything to bring in that new money." Ricky comment.

I grin.

"Mya, Rick, I like you to meet-,"

"Journey Calloway," both Ricky and Mya said. "Big fans, read your work."

"Thank you," I said, smiling.

"Journey, Mya is a fashion designer. Sunday Blues,"

"Yes!" I exclaim with excitement! "I love your clothing."

"Thank you," Mya said.

"And Ricky is here is in real estate," Nathan informs.

"Very nice," I said, smiling.

"Come on, come on," Victor said impatiently.

We laugh at his antsy and impatient demeanor. Within moments, we were on the field with our caddies not far behind.

AFTER WE PLAYED GOLF, we sit inside the lounge of the country drinking and eating appetizer-type finger foods, egg rolls, pretzel bites with spicy dipping cheese sauce, stuff shrimp, fried zucchini. There is plenty of food and alcohol. I am enjoying myself. This trip to the country club has been a pleasant distraction from my fight with LaKeya and my missing Marcus. (which he has attempted to call and text, but I refuse to answer either.) I am sitting in this beautiful country club that is cool and comfortable. I see beautiful black people, dark-skinned, brown-skinned, light-skinned, smiling, talking, and interacting with each other. No one seems pretentious or puffed up. I see the men smoking cigars, drinking Ciroc, and women drinking wine or Champaign. No one looks plastic or made; they look naturally beautiful.

The golf game was fun, mainly because I won and I actually laughed with Nathan and my new friends. Victor was very competitive during the game. Ricky and Mya didn't seem to care too much about winning, and Nathan actually gave Victor a run for his money, but I actually win.

We sit in the lounge in the seating area, laughing and enjoying ourselves.

"How long have you two been together?" Mya asks, referring to Nathan and me.

Awkward. I say to myself.

I nervously look at Nathan and then look back and, Mya and Ricky.

"Awe, we-," I stammer.

"We just started dating," Nathan smiled.

I smile, liking that answer.

"Are you enjoying yourself on The Island?" Ricky asks.

"Yes, sunshine, fresh air, pretty black people!" I exclaim.

I see people looking at me. I realize that I was too loud. Ricky, Nathan, Mya, and Victor laugh at my enthusiasm. The people looking at me smile at me.

"Sorry," I respond, feeling embarrassed.

"Don't be sorry, sister." One of the on-lookers said.

They raised their glasses to me to toast my jubilee. I raise my glass to them, thanking them for allowing them to be me. I look to my new friends.

"I have never seen such a beautiful Mecca," I said. "Rich black people of all shades."

"Oh yes, most of the people on The Island are considered The New," Mya informs. "This island was established for The New, but The Established comes here and tries to bring down the moral."

"Why?" I asked.

"For the obvious reasons." Mya answers. "The new money is to be considered social climbers."

Her comments sound like LaKeya's philosophy.

"I worked hard for my money," I say with defense.

"I know, sister," Mya says with her hands reach out to me.

I take in a deep breath.

"I'm sorry," I say. "A little post-traumatic stress disorder."

Nathan chuckles.

"In Journey's defense, she had been defending her success," Nathan says for me.

"We know your struggle," Mya said. "I have been a fan of yours since your first book. I am a fan. So I know that your struggle is real. Those who think you're just a fifteen-minute sensation are jealous of you. They don't have your heart."

I grin.

"Thank you," I say.

"You're welcome, Queen," Mya said, smiling. "As a matter of fact, I think you are beautiful, exceptionally beautiful. I would love for you to model Sunday Blues. There is a photoshoot this coming Saturday at noon if you don't have any plans."

As a matter of fact, this Saturday at approximately twelve noon is the christening for Isaiah and David. I shoot Nathan a quick look; he says nothing as he sips his Ciroc.

"I have no plans."

"Journ," Nathan says softly.

I pull out my cell phone and take down Mya's phone number. Once she gives me the phone number, I text her so she has my number. I smile.

"So tell me more about The Island." I request.

"Well, as mention, The Island is a place for us to vacation, instead of Martha's Vineyard or the Hamptons. " Ricky said.

"Martha's Vineyard is not so bad," I said.

"No," Victor begins. "but it's The Established territory. The Island is territory for The New; that is why Vision Campbell established The Island."

"What?" I ask.

I look at Nathan. He looks away.

"The Island, this beautiful resort, vacation spot for the richer and richer, was established by one woman?"

Victor nods his head. I look at Mya and Ricky, and they nod their hand.

"Okay, how did she establish this island?" I ask.

"Once she became successful as a model, she brought a piece of land and had it cleaned up, made roads and communities, and build homes?" I ask.

"Yes," Mya answered.

"It's not an obtainable goal," Nathan said.

"The Island is as big as a small state, Delaware!" I exclaim.

Everyone laughs.

"Yes, Vision throws weekly parties for The New." Victor also informed.

I look at every one. I suddenly realize that the people I am sitting with, talking to, and mingling with have something to do with Vision Campbell. I look at Victor.

"What do you do for Vision?" I ask.

"What do you mean?" Victor asks evasively.

"What is your connection to Vision Campbell?" I ask, a different way.

Victor looks away as if there is some kind of secret. He looks back at me.

"I am her business manager." He confesses.

My mouth is agape.

"Her manager?" I ask.

Victor nods his head.

"I plan those parties, organize her networking, photoshoots, and other business deals that she does," Victor tells me.

"I see," I reply.

I look at Ricky, I grin. He grins at me.

"What do you do, for Ms. Campbell?" I ask.

"She owns the land, and she and I own the homes." He says.

I nod my head.

"Okay, okay, okay," I said to him.

I look to Mya. It is not obvious what she does for Vision. I think of those pictures in the magazine where she is wearing pretty clothes.

"You dress her," I say.

Mya nods. I nod and then eat a shrimp. I look to Nathan. Other than being her friend or someone that she knows, Nathan never told me what his relationship is with Vision. I look at him, hoping that he will tell me what his connection to Vision is, but Nathan remains quiet. Hopefully, tonight, if there will be a tonight, he will tell me.

"I am renting her loft," I said.

"We know," Mya said, smiling. "We make a point to know all of the newbies on The Island, especially The New, newbies."

"Well, I am intrigued with who she is, how she became so successful. Have you seen the loft? It's like a beautiful place."

Mya nods her head with a smile.

"Yes, the loft is amazing, and you are very lucky to be renting it," Mya said.

"Will she be at the photo shoot?" I ask with a smile.

Mya shakes her head.

"It is evident that she is a recluse," Ricky said. "Vision is a complex individual."

I nod, excepting that answer, and look at the clock on the wall, and surprised at how late the hour is. We have been at the country club for a few hours. I feel a bit tired

82

and ready to leave, but I don't want to leave my new friends, and I hope to find more information about Vision Campbell. Why is she so reclusive?

I LAY IN BED, not able to sleep. I look to my left, and Nathan is sleeping soundly. I want to wake him and tell him that I want him to be awake because I am awake, but instead, I get out of bed, put on my robe, and walk to the patio to get some fresh air. I hear crickets singing in the background. I look up at the sky. It's a beautiful indigo blue that has been decorated with stars. The patio has large tropical trees that hide people from the world, almost like a fort; I feel safe and protected out here. It's surprisingly cool. I sit down in the chair and think about my day.

It started off well, I have an Island Boyfriend, someone that I can enjoy, but I don't want to engage in. He is temporary. He is here to scratch an itch, an itch that I had for some time. Not only does he scratch that itch, but he makes a good companion. Nathan is someone I can talk to, so it seems. I must admit, I am looking forward to spending the rest of the summer with him. I think about the fight with LaKeya how she changed. I know that life can change how we think and see things. I know life can change the outlook on things, but her view of me, her parents, and that Monica has done more than change. I think about what Ricky, Mya, and Victor told me regarding Vision Campbell, that she owns The Island and Ricky owns the property that they are renting, that rich and fabulous mansion. Booker has to know. I think about the idea of owning something so splendid, such as an island that is as big as a state and turning the island into some luxury resort. How much money does one need to have to own an island? I heard of celebrities owning islands in France or some kind of off-the-side country, but they do movies at ten million per movie. I don't want to underestimate Vision Campbell's finances, but how is all this possible.

I would like to own an island—some kind of destination or resort that people come to relax and unwind. I would like to have a property that people can rent, and I make money from their rental. Is that something obtainable for me? I think of the people that I admire, self-made millionaires. I think of the celebrities that conquered one area and dominated others, Jennifer Lopez, a dancing queen, then actress, then businesswoman, with her fragrances and clothing line. I think if I conquered the writing world. I have an established business with speaking engagement on how to self-publish and market. What else can I conquer?

"What are you doing up?"

I turn around and see Nathan. He looks good standing in a pair of pajama bottoms and no shirt. I smile at him—the diamonds in the sky highlight against his dark chocolate body.

"Hi," I said, smiling at him. "What time is it?"

"It's almost five a.m.," he answers.

I nod my head and look around.

"I couldn't sleep," I tell him.

"Oh yeah, why? That thing with you and Keya?" Nathan asks.

"Yeah, and what I learned about Vision Campbell?"

"What is with your obsession with Vision?" Nathan asks.

"Her, the elusiveness of her. Why is she so elusive?" I ask. "How did she become so successful?"

"Look at her," Nathan said. "She is what the world wants to see. She is light-skinned, with hazel-colored eyes."

"So because she is light-skinned, she is considered beautiful?" I asked.

"She captures that urban vibe with her dreadlocks," Nathan said.

"I have dreadlocks," I said.

"And I think you fly," Nathan said, playfully poking me in the stomach.

I laugh and playfully push his hand away.

"Seriously," I said, "How do you know her?"

Nathan still hesitates on telling me.

"I won't be jealous of you, and her were an item," I said.

"No, no," Nathan objects, frowning his face. "Nothing like that."

"Then what?" I question.

"Come inside," Nathan said.

Together we walk inside the loft. Nathan leads me back to the bedroom. The unmade bed looks comfortable. I climb in, and then Nathan climbs in after me. I hold onto a pillow as if I am at a slumber party and Nathan is going to tell me a scary story.

"Vision Campbell is my sister," Nathan says.

My mouth is agape.

"Your sister," I said.

"Yes, my adopted sister." Nathan said. "but she was there before me, so,"

"Tell me everything."

Nathan lets out a sigh.

"My parents struggled to have children, so they adopted a pretty baby, and within a year, I came. Because she looks almost odd, the skin, the eyes, the kinky hair, she was rejected most of her life."

"Is she mixed?" I asked.

"Yes, Vision found her real parent when she was about eighteen years old. Both sides rejected her; the black side rejected her because she was so light, and the white side rejected her because there was a hint of black in her. No one seemed to care. My sister got married to this guy; he was abusive. He was dark-skinned, and he married her for the sake that she looked white. It was the type of commission for him because she is that light. However, her beauty made him very, very insecure. He beat her up several times trying to destroy her face and self-esteem -,"

"Why didn't you help her?" I ask.

"Who says that I didn't?" Nathan scoffs, "I want to kill the man. Eventually, my family was able to get her away from him. She lived with me for a few years, and then at a party for a client of mine, she met Booker."

I nod my head.

"What happened with Booker and her?"

"Her pedigree," Nathan said. "Booker's family was adamant about him marrying a woman who comes from a good pedigree."

"LaKeya is from the projects!" I said.

"But my sister is adopted and rejected by her biological family. She has no background. My parents were both educated individuals, but that was not good enough for Booker's family. Plus, with a divorce on her record, to Booker's family, that is a no-no. They rather have LaKeya than Vision. Plus, like you said, LaKeya had been primed to be a rich man's wife. Vision is very open and opinionated; although she is reclusive, her voice is heard in other ways. Such as the very visual way she gets people's attention."

"By becoming a model?" I ask.

"Yes. My sister feels that every time someone sees her, they will know that she is a survivor. She only makes herself visible whenever there The Establish is around."

I nod my head.

"LaKeya knows nothing about Booker, and she?" I ask.

"No,"

"Did Booker love your sister?"

"I believe he did." Nathan answers. "But to stay in his family's money, Booker had to choose. Booker doesn't believe in his family's values, but he needs his family's money. This is why LaKeya acted the way she did; one snap of Booker's family's finger and LaKeys is dismissed. The twins are exactly what she needs to be cemented into Booker's family, but then again. If something was to ever go bad in their relationship, Booker's family can take the boys from LaKeya and raise them without her."

I gasp. It made sense as to why she felt like nothing more than Mrs. Booker Matthews. If Booker breaks things off, then LaKeya has nothing. I felt bad that I argued with her the way that I did, but I stand by my conviction regarding her family and her past.

I shake my head at the information that was given me.

"I find it ironic that the people you introduced me to today all work for Vision Campbell," I said. "Is there something I am supposed to do with Vision Campbell?"

"I don't know," Nathan said. "I mean, we are all friends. Victor, Mya, and Ricky."

"Can I meet her?" I ask.

"Why?" Nathan asks.

"Because I want to meet her. I want to see her in person, hear her voice."

Nathan yawns.

"I'll talk with her about it." He said.

"Fair." I said.

I find myself yawning.

"Come on," Nathan said. "Let's get some sleep."

5

I AWAKE TO THE smell of breakfast. I smile at the fact that Nathan is cooking. I get out of bed and into the bathroom to freshen up. I take a long hot shower, allowing the hot water to baptize me. I dress in pair of white Capri pants and a matching white top. My dreadlocks hang down my back. I walk into the kitchen and see the beautiful spread. I see fresh fruits, apples, peaches, plums, and grapefruit. I see bagels and cream cheese. I see Nathan cooking bacon, sausage, and eggs.

"Wow," I said.

Nathan turns around and smiles at me.

"You keep treating me right; I may get hooked on you." I teased, sitting down.

Nathan sets a cup of coffee down in front of me. I notice that he seemed distant.

"What's wrong?" I ask.

He puts the bacon, eggs, and sausage in front of me, and then he sits down. He seems solemn.

"Don't get mad," he begins.

"Okay," I say slowly.

"I invited LaKeya here, so you two can talk," Nathan confesses.

I nod my head, not sure if I am angry or okay with his idea.

"You two have been friends for years, a long time, a lifetime. One argument cannot break your relationship." Nathan said.

"Whatever," I say.

I grab grapefruit and sprinkle sugar on it and begin to eat. Then I sip my coffee.

"Does she know that Vision Campbell is your sister?" I ask.

"No," Nathan said. "All she knows is that Booker and I are friends from college."

I nod.

I place food on my plate, bacon, eggs, sausage, and more fruit. I am not in the mood to talk to LaKeya. I could care less if I never speak with her again. However, Nathan has a point. We are lifelong friends, and nothing should hinder that. I love her like the sister I never had, however in most families siblings fight, without repentance.

Within moments, I hear her car pull up to the loft, that pearl-colored Phantom. I hear her get out, and I hear her walk to the door and knock. I look at Nathan and then get up and answer the door.

"Hi," I say coolly.

"Hey," she replies.

I step aside for her to enter in, and then I shut the door. I walk back into the kitchen with her following me.

"Hey Key," Nathan says. "Want something to eat."

"Ah, sure." LaKeya answers.

"I'll leave you two alone," Nathan said.

I sit down to finish my breakfast. As Nathan leaves, LaKeya sets her purse, a royal blue Birkin, down in an empty chair. She grabs an empty plate and puts breakfast on the plate.

"Did you cook this?" she asks.

"No, Nathan did," I said, sipping my coffee.

"Oh," she says with a smirk.

LaKeya sits down and looks at me with a side-eye.

90

"When did that start?" she asks, smiling.

I shrug my shoulder, being evasive because I don't know how to elaborate on Nathan and I being an Island Item. Two, I am still mad at her and don't want to indulge in anything with her. LaKeya begins to eat. The silence is painful. The only noise that is heard is the forks hitting against the plates. She looks at me.

"I'm sorry, Journ." She says.

I nod my head accepting her verbal apology. However, I need more. I need her to tell me what her problem is or was. I know and understand, per Nathan, that she has to be on her P's and Q's best conservative behavior, or it is bye-bye Mrs. Matthews and hello LaKeya Jones. She has made nothing of her life outside of Booker. I know that if something happens, getting a job would be difficult, she never worked, and if Booker Matthews dumps her, then she would be considered worthless. However, I want her to tell me this, not an on-looker or an observer. I want her to tell me her insecurities. After all, we are best friends. That is my job to listen to her insecurities and be there for her.

"I don't know what came over me." She begins. "The stress of having the perfect christening for the boys. Everyone is going to be there."

"I know, that is a lot of pressure," I said.

"My parents are not as refined for an event like this. A lot of potential clients for the bank. I need perfection."

"Your parents are coming to bond with their grandsons. They could care less about those stuffy clients." I say.

LaKeya looks away from me, focuses on the scenery outside, and then she continues to eat. I can never tell that she will never admit to me her insecurities with Booker.

"Key, if you never married Booker, what would you be doing?" I ask.

"I don't know." She answers.

"You went to school for sociology. You know how people act and think. You can work with the youth from the bad neighborhoods and teach them that they can have a life like yours."

She shrugs her shoulders and puts a folk full of food in her mouth. I take that gesture as that she is not going to talk about the possibilities of a life outside of Booker.

"Not everyone is as blessed as you to take a hobby and make it a career." She says.

"No," I said, "but as women, we should not solely rely on their husbands. Always have a plan B., ya know."

"I guess, but I am okay." She says to me. "I want to tell you that I'm sorry. I want you as my children's godmother."

I look away. I made plans to spend with Mya at her fashion shoot. However, this is my lifelong friend.

"I'll be there," I said.

"Good," LaKeya said, smiling.

I really want to be at Mya's photoshoot instead of at LaKeya uptight, upscale christening.

"So, tell me about Nathan," she says, smiling.

I grin.

"No," I say quickly.

I stand and place my empty plate in the sink.

"Journey, come on! I tried to hook you up a few days ago, and you declined; now I am here, and he is here; what's going on?"

I shrug my shoulders and walk back to the table.

"I am enjoying my vacation," I say, being evasive.

"Okay, fine." LaKeya stands. "Will you come by tonight? We can have a nice dinner. You, Nathan, Booker, and me, just like the other day."

"I'll let you know," I answer.

"Okay,"

LaKeya says. She grabs her purse, and I walk her to the door. She turns around to face me.

"I am really sorry. Sometimes, I forget what is important. True friends are important; you are important."

"Thanks, Key," I grin.

She reaches for me and gives me a hug. I hug her back. This hug feels good because now I can accept her apology emotionally.

I watch LaKeya walk to her car, and she quickly drives off. I turn around to find Nathan standing behind me. He is smiling at me.

"I called Mya and told her that you can't make the fashion shoot."

"I really want to be there too," I said, frowning.

"I know, but there will be some kind of party afterward. We can go to that." Nathan said.

"Okay," I said, smiling.

"Cool, there is a beach party, east of The Island. Would you like to go?" Nathan asks.

"Of course!" I exclaim.

THE WEATHER IS HUMID; the sand looks like white diamonds. The water looks like a blue-topaz-colored pool. I hear the music playing, and I smell the barbeque. I lift my head to inhale the aroma of the atmosphere. I see beautiful black people, all different shades, light-skinned, brown-skinned, and dark-skinned, their melanin sparkling under the sun. I look at Nathan from behind my shades and smile at him; he smiles back.

"Nate!" I hear a familiar voice,

I look to the sound of the voice and see Victor. He is smiling at us, wearing bright color swimming trunks. He is smiling and waving at us. I laugh at Victor as he approaches us.

"Good thing, I am wearing my sunglasses," I teased. "Brotha, your trunks-,"

"Don't hate, baby girl!" Victor laughs.

Victor leans forward to kiss me on the cheek, and he shakes Nathan's hands.

"So, what is this party for?" I ask.

"This is a vacationing island. Do we need a vacation to party?" Nathan chuckles.

"Right," I said, smiling.

"Come on,"

Nathan takes me by the hand, and we follow Victor to a section that he is staying at. I see people dancing and eating, enjoying themselves. There are no formalities; everyone seems free and relax as they soak in the sun.

"Journey Campbell?!" Someone calls my name.

"Yes," I look around to see who is calling me.

It's a beautiful woman smiling at me. She is wearing a white swimsuit that looks like the old school swimsuits that the Hollywood legends wear. She has her hair worn in an afro, which I love as I look at her.

"I'm Sydney Baker. A fan, I love your books. I went to one of your seminars about building your business, Business Mind." She says to me, smiling.

I smile at her. Although I don't remember her, I smile at her anyway.

"Your seminar changed my life; after that weekend, I started my own consultant company." She said.

"Congratulations!" I exclaim.

"Thank you. I have million-dollar clients, and I once I heard that you were on The Island, I couldn't wait to officially meet you."

I extend my hand to her; she shakes it.

"It's a pleasure meeting you."

"Journ, I'm going to get a plate." Nathan interrupts, "Do you want anything?"

"No, I'm okay," I reply.

As Nathan leaves to get himself something to eat, I focus my attention back on Sydney.

"So, what type of consulting company do you run?" I ask.

"A branding consultant. I help people build their brand." Sydney answers.

I nod my head impressed with her company.

"It's called Sydney Baker Inc. or S.B.I., nothing fancy, but I help those starting their business establish their business, get the licenses, their logos, websites, and how to market."

I nod my head impressed.

"Journey, you really helped me make that leap, and I want to say thank you."

"You are more than welcome." I say smiling.

She shakes my hand again and then walks away. I stand for a moment, basking at the moment that someone's lives have changed because of my encouragement. Maybe I can do that with LaKeya. She acts as if she is a temp on a job, and she has ninety days to prove to her husband that she is worth being on the job full time. Never mind the fact that she carried not one but two babies. I know that she is a good wife, or do I? I never really saw her in wife action. Never saw her tend to details for Booker, other than this christening. I wonder what does a rich man's wife do? Are they trophy wives? On the arms of their men, smiling and shaking hands. During these events, do they speak when spoken to? Are all rich man's wives' socialites go to this event and that event, helping organize fundraisers and dinners?

Consider that Vision Campbell had hoped to be a rich man's wife; what would her life be if she married Booker. I look around at everyone on the beach. They seem so happy, partying and swimming, eating and dancing. I see a volleyball net set up and people playing. Would this island be here if Vision and Booker got married?

"JOURNEY!" Nathan says my name, pulling me from my thoughts.

"What, what?" I say, feeling embarrassed.

"Where are you?" he asks, laughing.

"I was caught up in this beautiful atmosphere." I lied.

He looks at me as if he doesn't believe me. I smile, hoping that he does believe me.

"I'm brainstorming," I confess.

"Really?" Nathan asks. "You may be writing something new?"

"I'm thinking about it."

Nathan sips his beer.

"Tell me; you heard enough about me, my life, my goals. Tell me something about you. Why did you become a sports agent?"

"I love sports. I love baseball, basketball, football, soccer, tennis, track and field, every sport. I tried to play them all, and I am more clumsy on the field than anything else, so I figured if I help those play the game, and can still be in the game, so to speak."

"Which clients are difficult to deal with?"

"The ones that want more money but don't have talent or have been benched because of an injury or because of some scandal."

I chuckle at that fact. I hear about it all the time. Athletes get into some kind of legal trouble. They would get suspended for at least a few games or the season, then want to demand more money. Or an injury has hindered their career, and they are forced to sit on the bench for the remainder of the season, and then when the doctors give them the okay to play, they want more money. And there is my favorite, the athlete that was the last pick in the draft round pick or they are third string on their team, but they have the nerve to request more money.

"What do you do with those clients?" I ask.

"Nothing," Nathan said. "Nine times out of ten, it's their attitude towards life that makes them seem like bad people. Arrogance, they think they are the stars they act a certain way towards people. Injuries, I feel bad because their injuries can hinder their careers, and they don't have a Plan

B. The Plan B's that they have, the money they would make, does not put a dent in the money they were used to, so they have to scramble on what to do. Their contacts are terminated, not getting that money."

Nathan shakes his head.

"What do you do for them?" I ask.

"There is nothing you can. At the risk of being selfish, I have to move on to an athlete whom I can bank on. I have to make money."

His comment is rough, but I have to respect it.

"Do you have a Plan B.?" I ask.

"Do you have Plan B?" he asks.

"I don't think I need a Plan B," I said. "My books will always sell; I book speaking engagements and writing seminars."

"Then no, I know, I don't have a Plan B.," Nathan said.

"Why don't you become a speaker? A type of motivational speaker. You can talk to potential athletes in high school and college the importance of having a plan B. An athlete is good up until a certain point. Football players have until the age of thirty before they are considered too old. Basketball players may be into their thirties, hockey players, baseball players. Teach them to have other business ventures they can make money from."

Nathan nods his head liking the idea.

"I can do that. Still make money." He said.

I smile.

"That is what you do?" He said.

"Yes, sometimes when I have writers' block and need a change of scenery, that is when I can make money on seminars or speaking engagement."

Nathan grins. I smile at him bashfully.

"You're amazing." He said to me.

I look at his surprise.

"Me amazing?" I ask. "Nathan, you don't know me?"

"Know you?" Nathan ask. "I spent nearly three days with you, and I have yet to want to go back to my hotel room and spend the rest of my vacation solo."

I stop walking and look at him.

"The company has been nice. Someone to hang out with during the day and someone to keep me warm during the night." I said with a smirk.

"The company has been nice," Nathan said, smiling.

"You been more of a therapist instead of an Island Item," I joke.

We continue to walk along the beach.

"An Island Item," he laughs.

"Yes," I said. "You help LaKeya and me settle our argument."

"Would have called her if I didn't?"

I think for a moment. The right thing to do would be to call, to say: "I'm sorry," and to hope that we can get past the argument. We are talking nearly twenty-five years of friendship, a type of sisterhood. I nearly fought a woman because of her comments towards her parents, who are like parents to me. Although LaKeya and I are not in touch like we used to, she didn't hesitate to make me the godparents of her children. However, would I have called, considering how rude and mean she has been? The past few days, she has been condescending, causing me to feel like I need to validate my worth to her. Spending the summer here and not speak with LaKeya could be a long summer.

I would maybe see her at the Island Club and force myself to speak. It would be a painful conversation, trying to make pleasantries. One's pride would be to prove that we are having a fabulous summer without the other. I wouldn't want that. My goal this summer was to spend with my oldest and dearest friend, eating colossal shrimp and grilled scallops, soaking up the sun, and buying expensive clothes so when I go back to New York, I can be the black Carrie Bradshaw.

"I don't know, Nathan." I finally answered. "What I do know is that she ticked me off. She belittled me so far, and this vacation is barely a week old. I have another two months to go. Considering what you have shared with me, I am not sure that I can stomach *this* LaKeya. The LaKeya I knew would not have tolerated a woman like Monica. *She* would have seen right through her and cut her down like the little woman that she is. LaKeya liked the finer things. She likes Champaign and diamonds, she is very Chanel, but she was genuine and warm."

"I think that you and LaKeya would have made up and gone acting like nothing has happened," Nathan said.

"That is what you men do." I scoff. "Us women, when we get mad, we stay mad."

Nathan laughs.

"This is true," I said. "Speaking of LaKeya, she wants us to come to the mansion, you and me tonight."

"I think it would be great," Nathan said.

"Booker and I can play pool, talk politics, and drink while you ladies gossip and drink," Nathan said with a chuckle.

"Okay, okay," I let out a sigh. "The scenery on the patio is beautiful. Looking over the lake under the stars at night. I am sure that she and I can get past our issues and move forward. Maybe, just maybe, I can convince her to believe that she doesn't need Booker. So if something was to happen, she be okay."

Nathan nods his head. I realize that he has been very supportive in LaKeya's relationship. For someone who is just an Island Item, I find that sweet and kind but somewhat alarming.

"Nate, why are you so invested in this?" I ask.

"No reason." He said. "I hate seeing a good friend lose their friendship over something stupid. I care about you both."

"Okay, and with regards to your sister," I ask rhetorically.

"Here is the thing," Nathan begins. "How Booker dropped my sister was cold. Because of his family's issues, my sister has a broken heart. She has dedicated her life to get back and to make sure that The New is never shamed or looked down apart, but I do hope for your friend's sake that he doesn't allow his family to do the same to her because, with regards to you, she can dismiss you because of his family."

"Again, I ask you," I begin, "Why are you friends with someone him?"

"I'm an idealist. I hope that one day, he will stand up to his family, just like you, believe that one-day LaKeya will see her worth."

I take in a deep breath. I am starting to get a headache. The beauty of the beach is starting to irritate me. The melanin that surrounds me is starting to blend in together, looking like a beautiful bronze blend of people. The sunlight is so bright that it makes the diamond-colored sand sparkle forcing my eyes to hurt, and the blue topaz-colored ocean is making me sleepy. So far, during this beach party, I have eating more than my fair share of shrimp, grilled vegetables, and drank enough wine to sleep for two days.

"Well, take me home; I am starting to get nauseous. I need to take a nap. Maybe when I wake up, I'll feel better."

I ARRIVE IN THE loft; the cool air from the central air conditioner is welcoming. I breathe in the cool air and tilt my head back. Quickly I remove my clothes and throw them on the floor and climb into my bed. Nathan said he would come by and take it to LaKeya's and Booker's around five p.m. I close my eyes and allow the sleep to consume me.

There has been a lot that has happened; it a matter of days. The argument with LaKeya and me, Vision Campbell and Nathan are brother and sister, and she owns The Island. She wants emotional revenge on Booker, and there is Nathan and me. I will say since I have been on The Island, I have yet to really think about Marcus. I have somehow escaped the mental and emotional abuse that I once accepted for the sake of having a man, and now I have an Island Commitment with my Island Item. Knowing that this will end at the end of the summer is somewhat liberating. I am under no obligation to be his only woman, no more than he is under no obligation to be my only man. In a strange way, I like it because technically, I am not here on The Island for him, I am here for me, and even if we don't last through the duration of this vacation, I can say with honesty that it's all good. Nathan so far has become a good friend. He seems to be a good man, and if he was my permanent man, I would be happy. He seems easy to talk to. I wonder why he doesn't have a girlfriend, or does he? Does he have a woman at home waiting for him to return, and I am just someone he needs to spend time with so he is not technically alone. However, why do I care? He is just an Island Item.

My thoughts lead me to my subconscious. I dream of Vision Campbell and Booker. I wonder what their lives were like when they dated. I see a pretty woman with auburn colored hair in long Goddess Locs, Lisa Bonet style. Her hazel-colored eyes sparkle every time she looks at him and when he smiles at her. I see a young, handsome man dressed in fine silks bestowing diamonds and pearls, flowers, and clothes, making her feel beautiful and wonderful, especially considering what she has been through from her marriage. I see them taking photos together, looking like the perfect couple, The Prince of the Bank and the Princess of Beauty. I can see them; her beauty exudes through the photos. Everyone wants to know who she is and where did she come from?

I see him whispering in her ears that he will be that Knight in Shining Armor, rescuing her from the evil dragon of rejection, rejection from her parents, rejection from her ex-husband. I can see Vision in Booker's home being the lady of the house. She is wearing beautiful clothes wearing diamonds and pearls, sitting elegantly at the table in a seat entertaining Booker's friends and clients. She would win them over with her beauty and charm. And once these clients become clients of Bookers and decide to bank with Matthews Bank of America, again he would adorn her with more jewelry, more clothes, and more love.

However, I see the end; I see him taking her by the hand while sitting in a beautiful restaurant. I see Vision's eyes light up because she thinks that he is going to propose. Booker is going to ask her to marry him, with tears in her eyes, forcing her eyes to look like a citrine stone. She will say yes. She holds her breath, waiting for those words to come out:

"Will you marry me?"

But instead, Booker tells her.

"We have to go our separate ways." He says coolly.

Booker shows no emotion. He doesn't look upset or happy, just a stoic. Those words catch Vision off guard. She gasps at the words, thinking that she missed heard him, but he takes his hand away from hers.

"What, why?" I hear her say.

I see her shaking her head, trying to make sense at what was just said. It came out of nowhere. Booker coolly shrugs his shoulders, not giving her an explanation. He gets up from the table and leaves her there alone, shocked, stunned, and embarrassed.

She goes home to Nathan and tells him what happened. Nathan asks why and what happened. She tells him, she tells how he left her alone at the restaurant. She sobs hysterically in Nathan's arms.

"Why doesn't anyone want me?" I hear her asks. "What is wrong with me?"

"Is going to be okay," Nathan says, to her holding her. "He did you favor."

A few days later Nathan meets up with Booker to find out what happened. He wants to punch Booker in the face, but fighting won't heal his sister's broken heart.

Booker seems arrogant when questioned about why he broke up with Vision.

"It's between her and me," Booker says coolly.

"My sister is crying and starving herself, thinking something is wrong with her! I need you to explain to me what happened." Nathan demands.

Nathan approaches Booker. His subtle yet aggressive approach is somewhat intimidating to Booker.

"My parents don't feel like she is someone I want to surround myself with," Booker confesses.

"Excuse me?" Nathan questions.

"Her background," Booker said. "Your sister doesn't have a qualifying pedigree. My parents want me to marry someone with a better pedigree."

"My parents are upstanding individuals." Nathan defends.

"Yes, but your sister, she's adopted, rejecting from both sides of her biological family. That can bring questions unwanted questions. Plus, she is divorced, another questionable topic that can hinder the family business."

What Booker said is unfathomable. It's sad and heartbreaking.

"Booker, you are a good man. You have a reputable reputation. You are not shallow." Nathan said. "You possibly can't mean what you are saying."

"Nathan, I need my family's support. If they don't support me, I can lose everything."

"Then build your own business." Nathan admonishes.

Booker shakes his head and takes a swallow of his drink.

"It's not that easy. You were not raised in the type of family that I was raised in. You were raised by blue-collar people that believed in working hard, paying dues, and everything will work out. I was raised in the white-collar, where it was we worked hard, we paid those dues, now you do as I say."

"My sister is heartbroken because of your family's bigotry," Nathan says.

"I'm sorry, Nathan, but I can't. I don't have a choice." Booker says.

Nathan then realizes that there is nothing he can do to save his sister from a broken heart. He looks at Booker and realizes that he is just a little boy that is forced to do what his mommy and daddy tell him. Nathan nods his head as to consent to defeat.

"Nathan, please don't let this be the end of our friendship," Booker says.

"Do you think I can look you in the eyes or allow you to look me in my eyes, knowing that you crushed my sister's dreams and feelings?"

"No, that wouldn't be fair to either of us,"

Nathan turns around and walks out of the house. He returns to Vision; she was standing at the window looking like an epic princess wrapped in a white blanket, wearing a pair of white wide legs pants and a white tank top. She turns to face Nathan as he enters the room, and Nathan tells her,

"Per Booker's family, you are not good enough," he says bluntly.

"I am not good enough?" she questions. "Did I say, 'can I instead of may I?' Did I use the wrong fork at the dinner table? Did I used the word ain't instead of isn't?"

Nathan shakes his head.

"It's your background, you being adopted and divorced," Nathan said.

Vision Campbell nods her head like Nathan did in Booker's mansion, accepting the defeat.

"I am destined to be nothing." She says solemnly.

"No," Nathan said. "You are born to win."

"How?" she asks. "How? No one wants me."

"So make them want you!" Nathan states. "It's wasn't by accident that you were born beautiful. Make them see you, own the world. They will have no choice but to come through you."

Immediately I sit up and realize that Nathan is the backbone to Vision Campbell's success. He is not Booker's friend because Booker is a nice guy, but he is Booker's friend, so every time Booker looks at Nathan, it is a clear reminder of what he did to Vision, and it's the window that Vision needs to show herself as success. She is a haunting image to Booker. I wonder if Booker knows that she owns The Island? Or was it Nathan's idea to vacation here, so Vision gets her rental fees. Mya, Ricky, and Victor are they in connection with Vision's revenge?

I look at the clock and see that it was about four-thirty. I slept and dreamed of Vision Campbell. I want to talk with her more than ever. I want to know her. She has transformed her heartache into a gold mine.

Quickly I shower and dress. I refuse to find something perfect to wear to LaKeya's. I wear an aquamarine-colored sundress a pair of gold ballerina-styled flat shoes. I pull my dreadlocks into a bun and wear aquamarine-colored pearl earrings and a matching necklace. I feel good. I do a soft subtle makeup, aquamarine-colored eye shadow with gold highlights, soft, not overdone. I hear Nathan is knocking on the door. I walk to the door to answer it and smile at him as he stands on the other side. He looks just as cool and comfortable, a pair of khaki slacks and a white polo shirt.

"You look amazing." He says to me.

He enters the house and leans forward to kiss me. I kiss him back our kissing gets passionate. I am caught off guard.

"What was that about?" I ask.

"No reason." He answers.

I nod my head accepting his romantic yet cool approach towards me.

"Ready?" he asks.

"Yes,"

We get inside his car. I can't but think about my dream and the revelation that I had learned or think I had learned. After all, it was just a dream but was that dream my subconscious' way to tell me what is really the truth? I want to say something to Nathan, but I don't want to keep bringing up Vision Campbell. I want to enjoy my Island Fling, and he continues to enjoy me.

"How did you sleep?" he asks.

"Really good," I answer.

"Oh, yeah, you look refresh." He replies.

"As oppose to me looking ran over?" I suggest laughing.

"No," Nathan laughs. "You are beautiful, amazing, but I can tell that you had a lot on your mind, and you were not resting."

"Me having a lot on my mind has nothing to do with me not resting; it's you and the good sex that you deliver."

"Really?" Nathan says with a smirk.

I can see that he is trying not to smile like the Cheshire cat. So I have a big smile on my face for him.

"You know you're good," I say, smiling. "The best I had."

"Well, thank you," Nathan said, stealing a look at me as he drives. "I will say, it is a pleasure being with you as well."

"Oh, yeah?" I ask.

"Yes, why do you think I spend some much time with you?" He asks with a chuckle.

"So it's just for the sex?" I ask in a joking way.

"No, not just for the sex," Nathan defends himself.

"Relax, relax, it was a joke. I know what's going on."

"What's going on?" Nathan asks.

"That we are here for each other for the summer," I said. "No strings attached."

Luckily we come to red light, and Nathan looks at me, his eyes intense.

"Is that okay with you?" he asks.

"Yes," I tell him. "It's perfect, actually."

"Perfect?" he questions.

"Yes, perfect," I reply.

Nathan looks at me long and hard, as long as that red light allows. His look is making me nervous.

"What?" I ask.

"Can I ask why it's perfect?" he questions.

"Because I don't do well in committed relationships, so I've learned," I answer.

The light turns green, and Nathan drives.

"So you thrived on a non-committed relationship?" Nathan asks, sounding condescending.

"I guess because I am having more fun and better sex with you than I did in the relationships that I thought has some kind of promise. Maybe it's because there are no pressures; we're just enjoying ourselves, living in the moment."

"Okay," Nathan said.

The coolness behind his response is now alarming.

"Did I say something wrong?" I ask.

"No," Nathan said, quickly glancing at me.

"I just don't want to seem like a jerk when the summer is over, and we go back to our lives," Nathan said. "I like you. I see that you take relationships personally and-,"

"Let's make a pack." I begin. "Let's promise each other that after the summer, we stay friends, no matter what. We are godparents; any monumental thing that happens in the boys' lives will be there. So let's be mindful to always be friends."

Nathan looks at me with a grin.

WE ARRIVE AT THE mansion and are escorted to the sitting room by the butler. LaKeya stands and greets me with open arms. Booker smiles and hugs me.

"So glad that we got these girls back together," Booker says to Nathan, smiling. "Journey, LaKeya was so upset about the argument yesterday that she cried the whole day."

"Is that so?" I said, smiling at LaKeya.

LaKeya rolls her eyes at me in a playful way, but I know that Booker is probably telling the truth. I shoot

110

Booker a look and shake my head. I wonder if he laughed at her because of our argument. I sit down in the big chair and see the shrimp cocktail on the coffee table. I take a shrimp and put on in my mouth.

"Booker, when are your parents coming?" I ask. "I am dying to actually meet them."

"Actually, my parents are not coming," Booker informs as he hands Nathan a glass of Ciroc.

"What?" I asked, shocked.

Booker shrugs as if his parents not coming to their first grandchildren's christening is not a big deal. At the risk of having another argument with the etiquette of parents, I refuse to speak on the issue. I look to Nathan as he sits beside me.

"I hear that you two have been enjoying your summer," Booker says, smiling.

He looks silly as he smiles, like Dr. Evil in the *Austin Powers* franchise. Nathan and I share glances at how simple Booker looks, trying to confirm our relationship.

"So, LaKeya, how are the christening plans coming?" I ask, changing the subject. "Do you need any assistance with anything?"

"Probably arranging the flowers properly in the dining hall." She says. "Roses and gardenias, on the table as centerpieces. I would like all white, with a hint of lavender."

"Lavender as in the color of lavender as in the plant?" I ask.

"Lavender as in the plant to give a pop of color." She says, smiling.

I smile at her. This christening celebration is going to be very beautiful.

"There will be fireworks," Booker informs.

"Oh wow, that will be nice," I said.

"They are going to spell out the boys' name."

"That would be so adorable!" I said, smiling.

"I was thinking, Journey," LaKeya begins. "That Obama Glam dress that you brought at Christina's a few days ago, I don't think it's appropriate for the christening."

"Why?" I ask.

"The coloring is all." She answers with a shrug. "I thought that since you and Nathan are the godparents, that you two wear something cream colored with a hint of lavender. Booker and I are wearing white, with lavender as well. We are somewhat set apart."

"Okay," I say.

"Journey, we can pay for your dress if need be," Booker says to me.

"I can afford a new dress," I said to Booker with a grin.

Booker grins.

"Of course you can," Booker says, sipping his drink.

"Maybe we can go shopping tomorrow," LaKeya suggest.

"Sure," I reply.

The butler enters the sitting room.

"Dinner is served." He announces.

Together the four of us walk outside the sitting room and onto the patio. We see the table lit with cream-colored candles, a white table cloth, and a beautiful table setting. Dinner was lobsters with seasoned rice and a salad and an endless amount of Champaign. Like the first time I was here, the scenery is beautiful. The sun is beginning to set. The coral-colored sun makes the lake behind us look like a pool of citrine and garnets. I want to take my clothes off and dive in the water, searching for the gemstones. Knowing what I know of Vision Campbell, I wouldn't be surprised if there were citrine and garnets stones inside the water. There is a bouquet of flowers as a centerpiece, the roses, gardenias, and lavender.

"See, the idea, Journ?" LaKeya asks as Nathan pulls the chair out for me.

"Yes," I said, smiling. "It looks beautiful."

I watch as Booker does not pull a chair out for LaKeya, and I watch as Booker seems distracted on his phone.

"So, how are you enjoying The Island?" Booker asks me.

"I am enjoying myself very well," I answered. "I have met some awesome, awesome people."

"Oh, like who?" LaKeya asks.

Inform LaKeya and Booker of Mya.

"She actually asked me to model for her this Saturday," I said.

"You declined, of course," LaKeya asks.

"Of course," I answer.

LaKeya grins at me.

"I have a make-up artist coming as well to make sure our make-up is flawless," LaKeya said. "A lot of potential clients are coming; if they invest or a bank with Booker, that will be real promising."

"There is a lot to getting those clients, huh, Booker?"

"Yes." Booker answers. "It's hard work because they can always bank elsewhere, and we need their business."

"Are most of your clients blacks?" I ask.

"Oh yes, it's important as one of the most powerful banks in American that African-Americans run that most of the clients are black. How foolish would it be if we didn't have African- American clients?"

"Booker is considering donating to the next Democrat running for office," LaKeya said proudly.

"Oh yeah?" I ask, smiling.

"Yes, that will also bring clients for Booker," LaKeya said proudly.

"Pretty soon, African-Americans will rule the world!" Booker said, raising his glass up as toast.

"Do you think so?" I ask.

"Absolutely," Booker said. "Nathan, tell me you agree."

Nathan chuckles, with hopes to avoid the subject, but Booker presses the issue.

"Just think nearly a hundred years ago, blacks had to beg to be accepted. We had incredible talent. Think, Josephine Baker, Sammy Davis Jr., that was entertainment, in the political realm, there was Shirley Chisholm, of course, W.E. B. DuBois, in modern times, Michael Jackson, Barak Obama, now there is a man that came out of nowhere, and now his name is a reference of opulence, of decadence, he is the epitome of the American Dream, and you Journey."

"Me?" I ask, caught off guard

"Yes, you!" Booker said. "You created a life that you were not born into."

"I may not have been born with a silver spoon in my mouth, but it is evident that I was ordained for greatness," I said proudly. "Just like, LaKeya."

"No, no, no," Booker says with a chuckle.

"Excuse me? I ask. "Why not?"

"It was me marrying her that gave her the clout that she has," Booker says coolly.

I shoot LaKeya a look. I can feel my blood pressure rising. She looks away, embarrassed that this fact is true, but I know better.

"Actually, it's the woman like LaKeya is why all those fancy people are coming to see you this weekend."

Booker scoffs as if my comment was laughable.

"Who is coordinating this event? Not you. Who is charming your friends and potential clients, not you? As a matter of fact, my sister here has been raised to be the type of woman on your arm."

Booker looks at LaKeya, his eyes intense and seeming angry as if she was the problem. I look at LaKeya. I want her to defend herself. I want her to stand up to Booker, letting him know that she doesn't need him to be successful. However, she sits back in her seat and slowly drinks her Champaign. I can see tears well up in her eyes.

"Book, relax," Nathan says in a soft tone.

"Relax," Booker says with a chuckle. "Relax. I will tell you about relaxing. You know something, Journey, you should be grateful that we asked you to be the godparents of my sons. That also gives you credibility in this world."

"What world are you talking about?" I asked. "You just compliment my strategy of obtaining the American Dream."

"Our world, the white-collar word, The Established." Booker says, his mouth frowned up as if he was "the man,"

"Booker," LaKeya says softly.

"Key, baby, it's okay," I say to her and then wink. "Listen, brother; I don't need to belong to The Established because I am the epitome of established. I own everything; you work for your parents."

Booker jumps up as if to attack me, immediately Nathan jumps up to guard Booker against me. I jump, ready to take him on, and LaKeya jumps up because she is scared. I am not sure what is going on or why. I don't understand why I am living this moment. My best friend's husband is volatile and mean.

"Booker, come on!" Nathan exclaimed. "We are trying to have a healthy and happy dinner. The girls made up, let talk about this christening, let's talk sports, let's not condemn each other."

Nathan, the peacemaker. I look at LaKeya. She grins at me. I hold my breath waiting for her to say: "Journey, let's go, take me to your loft. I am leaving Booker."

Booker takes a deep breath. He looks at me; I look at him. He looks at Nathan.

"Journey, I'm sorry." He says coolly. "LaKeya, I'm sorry."

I watch as Booker leans to the side and gives LaKeya a kiss on the cheek. She seems to relax a bit. I look at Nathan, and together with all four of us, sit down.

I don't understand this life. I don't understand why do I compete with individuals proving my worth. It's their insecurities because they really haven't accomplished anything, and they are jealous of those who have did? I worked hard for my success; why do I constantly feel as if I need to defend myself. It's not like I am some type of reality star that makes money from being glamorous. I am a writer, that turned their passion and hobby into a full fledged business. I teach how to write, how to market, how to strategize. I thought coming here to The Island would be perfect. It seems like each minute I am here, I have to prove myself. Did I make a mistake by coming here? Should I have gone to Africa, Paris, or Rome for my summer vacation?

As I sit and continue to eat and make painful idle conversation, I think about Vision Campbell. If I was to ever meet her, I would tell her that Booker did her a favor. If she married Booker, he would treat her like crap, and she be sitting her hating herself more than she has ever hated herself. As I sit and continue to eat, I can see that Booker is insecure to anyone who appears to be more powerful to him. Without his parents' money, he would not be on this island. He is handsome, but only by default, meaning that he has the money to be well-groomed. He has money to wear fancy suits. However, after knowing what I know and seeing what I saw, he is an ugly person. I feel sorry for my godsons. To have a father that is so ugly is discouraging. They need to know that they can make it in life without the aid of the family's money. I will personally invest money so they know they have something available when ready to merge out in the world.

AFTER THE DISASTROUS DINNER, we somehow managed to move back into the sitting room. More drinks have been served dessert, such as cheesecakes, carrot cake and some kind of moose are placed in the sitting room for us to eat. We finalize how the christening is going to be. It is going to almost like a wedding.

Booker and LaKeya will march down the aisle of the church, each carrying a baby while Nathan I are already standing at the front of the church with the reverend. The guest, of course, is already seated but will be standing as Booker, LaKeya and the twins come down the aisle. After the christening, we will take photos of mother and babies, then father and babies, and then mother, father, and babies. Dare I ask if LaKeya's parents will get the opportunity to take a photo with their grandsons? Then photos will be with godsons and me Nathan and godsons and then Nathan and me and godsons. During the reception dinner, there may be some photos taken with the potential clients and the babies. Finally, the press will be there to take more photos and get interviews with Booker and LaKeya.

I have never experienced a christening so grand. The christenings that I have been to have been at a church, the baby in a lovely christening gown or in the cuties little three-piece suit. The godparents are standing up next to the parents agreeing with their pledge to be the best godparents. Then for dinner, some kind of salmon or chicken serves with sparkling cider and some kind of marble cake. Friends and family will be taking pictures on their cell phones, laughing with each other, and enjoying themselves.

I need a moment alone with LaKeya to ask her, "What is going on?"

However, I know I just can't sneak her away. Maybe during our time shopping tomorrow, I can put a bug in her ear that will strike her heart. I am starting to get tired. It could be the alcohol or the fact that Booker is a complete moron.

"It's after midnight," I announced.

"Oh, come on, Journey, give us another hour." Booker teases. "You can't wait to get home to indulge in passion."

I take a deep breath.

"Classy, Book," I comment.

"I'm sorry, I'm sorry." Booker teases.

"Key, tomorrow at ten?" I ask, suggesting a time to go shopping.

"Sure."

I look to Nathan, and he quickly stands and holds his hand out to me. I take it to stand up. LaKeya and Booker stand. I walk to LaKeya and embrace her with a hug. I hold her tight, and she hugs me tight.

Oh yeah, we're going to talk. I say to myself.

I approach Booker, and we shake hands. I smile at him. Nathan kisses LaKeya on the cheek and shakes Booker's hand.

NATHAN AND I WALK inside my loft. We don't talk on the way back. As Nathan and I enter the loft, I walk to the master bedroom, sliding out of my shoes. Nathan is standing behind me. I look at him as he sits down on the bed. I want to run into his arms, he takes my dress off, and we have our passion, our Island Passion. In our world, we are free; there is no The New or The Established; we can escape the world around us and live in our world, The Free.

As I look at Nathan, I have to know if he helped Vision Campbell orchestrate the biggest revenge, to own The Island, and to make Booker pay for his vacation here.

"You're Booker's friend; explain tonight," I ask.

"I honestly don't know," Nathan said, unbuttoning his shirt.

He stands as he takes his shirt off and allows his shirt to fall on the floor. I lick my lips at his chocolate brown chest, waiting on the right time to lick every inch of that chest.

"He really feels like that about LaKeya, that she is nothing without him?" I ask. "If he dismisses her like he did your sister, she will break! I know her."

"She knows that," Nathan said. "Your friend is not stupid, just insecure. Seriously this is the life she wants. The world knows that Booker is a bastard! I know it, you know it, she knows it. She wants this life; she wants to be Mrs. Booker Matthews. So let her; let her. When she is ready, she will leave him."

"You think she will leave him?" I ask.

"She's your friend. What do you think?" Nathan asks.

"I don't know because she is not the friend that I grew up with. Yes, she wanted to be married to a rich man, but not a rich man that is emotionally or mentally abusive."

Nathan shrugs. I want to reveal my secret about what I know of him and his sister, but as he slowly approaches me, I know now is not the time to question my theory. He stands in front of me. I put my arms around his shoulders. Nathan leans down and kisses me passionately, taking my mind from Booker and LaKeya. As he kisses me, he slides his hand up my dress and caresses my butt, and pulls me into him. I can feel his passion. I moan as we grind slowly. Nathan unzips my dress, allowing it to fall to the floor. I stand before him in my strapless light blue bra and matching thong.

He takes his index finger and glides it along with my breast and down my stomach, and along my panty line.

I close my eyes, enjoying his touch. I want more of him. I want him more than I ever wanted a man. I unbuckle his belt and then unbutton his pants, and they slide on the floor, and within moments he steps out of his pants. He lifts me up in his arms and carries me to the bed, and soon we unit. He moves with slow yet strong strokes, causing me to moan with each thrust. I hear him moan softly. He kisses me passionately as we move together in sync. We roll over, and I am on top; I sit up on top of him and move my hips slowly. As I ride him, his hand rubs along my body, my breast. And as we climax, he calls my name:

"Journey," he says.

"Nathan," I said softly, reaching a full level of ecstasy that I have never reached.

I lie on his chest and listen to his heartbeat. He gently rubs my back.

"Hey," he says softly.

"Yes," I respond.

"That was really good." He says to me.

"Yes,"

I sit up and look at him. I look into his eyes; he has beautiful dark brown eyes that seem warm and welcoming.

"You're amazing." He says.

I lean in and kiss him.

"When you said that you don't do well in committed relationships," Nathan begins. "Why is that?"

"Ask them," I chuckle. "I tried to be that girl for my so-called boyfriends, but they didn't want me."

Together we sit up. I didn't want to talk about my past boyfriends to whom I assume is my lover. I want to bask in the passion and in ten minutes, indulge in more, hoping that he will take me to a higher ecstasy.

Nathan cups my face in his palm and passionately kisses me.

"I don't understand why those men in your life allowed you to get away." He says to me.

"It doesn't matter," I say. "In a sense, I am like your sister."

"Oh, how so?" he asks.

"Every time they look up, they see me, winning, making the best sellers list."

Nathan chuckles at the idea.

"I'm featured in the paper wearing Balmain, looking like a queen," I say, smiling with pride.

Nathan chuckles at my comment.

"But, I don't set out to show them up, but it does so happen that they happen to see me and miss me."

"Do you give them a second chance?" Nathan asks.

"No," I said. "Well, there was one-,"

I stop talking.

"Why did you stop talking?" Nathan said.

"I don't want to talk about it, them, with you."

"Talk to me," Nathan encouraged.

I shake my head. I lean and kiss him, passionately hoping to ignite him, I did, and we submerge ourselves in the bed. Again, like before, Nathan takes my body to a level that I have never experience. I know that we are not making love, but the way he holds me kisses me, has sex with me, feels like making love. I know that I am going to miss this when the summer is over. I know that the men from my past have never taken my body to the level of ecstasy that Nathan has taken me and is taking me. Often I have wondered why he is so nice to me, considering that this relationship is only for a season. What is he getting out of this deal? I know that I don't in the slightest miss Marcus. I don't miss any intimate times with Marcus, and compared to Nathan, Marcus is moot. I love the way Nathan kisses, the way he looks at me when he understands my issues, I love the way he moves with me. As we have sex, I look up at him; he looks down at me and smiles,

"You are so amazing," he says.

I put my arms around his shoulders, rubs his arms, and then he leans down to kiss me. Within moments we reach our high point; again, like a few moments ago, he calls out my name, and I call out his name. We lay in each other's arms, nothing wanting to move, our bodies tingling from the passion.

I DON'T REMEMBER FALLING asleep, but I wake up to the sun shining on my face. I sit up and see Nathan still asleep next to me. I smile. I go into the bathroom and take a shower. I decided to fix Nathan breakfast, considering that he fixes me breakfast. Plus LaKeya said that she would be here by ten. Nathan enters the kitchen and smiles as he sees me.

"Morning," he says.

"Good morning," I said, smiling.

"You are glowing." He says, wrapping his arms around me.

"Well, last night, you took ten years of stress off my life." I tease.

"I must say you were very enlightening as well." He says.

Nathan sits down as I hand him a plate loaded with pancakes, sausage patties, and I make hot grits.

"Wow," he says.

I shrug.

"I'm not just a freak in the bedroom, I am a chef in the kitchen as well," I say, with a wink.

"Well, all right." Nathan laughs.

We sit down, and we eat breakfast. I look at him, enjoying the scenery—a beautiful chocolate brown man eating breakfast with me. Nothing is forced or required—just two friends enjoying sex at night and breakfast in the morning.

"So, what are your plans while Keya and I go shopping?"

"I have to make some calls to my client and find a suit for this show of a christening." Nathan answers. "Maybe afterward, we go out to dinner. I know of a good, great seafood restaurant that serves fresh seafood and white wine, garlic bread."

"Hmm," I moan for the garlic bread.

"Sounds like a plan," I reply, smiling.

6

WE BARELY TALK ON the way to Christina's Boutique. There is definitely an elephant in the Maybach, a huge big elephant, riding in the back seat. I almost don't want to go to Christina's; I have a pretty white summer dress hanging in the closet, I can find some lavender colored jewelry on this beautiful tropical paradise, kiss my godsons, and be done with this whole thing, but to appease my oldest and dearest friend, and her delusional husband, I will get a dress that makes me look like a lonely bride's maid and parade with my godsons in my hands as if this is the social event of the season.

Since we have been en route, we have tried to make conversation, which has been painful.

"The weather is beautiful," LaKeya says.

"Yes, it is," I reply.

The weather is either beautiful or raining; this is a tropical island, for crying out loud. Unless it's my way of thinking, this is something beautiful about a tropical storm, not necessarily a horrific category five hurricane, the gray clouds and the tropical trees bending because of the forcefulness from the winds. The sound of the rain can be melodious, and the smell from a tropical island rain is a fresh aroma. So far, there has been no rain on The Island. Every morning, the sky has been clear, with the exception of the diamond-like sun in the sky. The humidity has been rough, but I love humid weather; for me, the warmer, the better. When it's too hot, I can consume myself in a cool pool and bake, returning to dry land looking like an eight ball or a rich cup of hot black coffee.

"I hear the weather is going to be beautiful for the christening," LaKeya informs.

"Good," I respond. "With all this white, we don't want the wind to kick up dust destroying our clothes."

"How do you plan on wearing your hair?" LaKeya asks.

"Considering the style of the event and depending on the dress, I would probably pin-up with a few bejeweled bobby pins, a little Audrey glam."

LaKeya nods her head. I know that she hates my dreadlocks. The idea that my hair is nappy and free goes against her well-groomed nature, but I love the freedom of my dreadlocks. Our parents made LaKeya and me believe that we were not together if our hair wasn't neat. However, I feel that for years black Americans or African-Americans have allowed themselves to be conformed to the European standard of beauty. In other black people need to look and present themselves the way white people feel is appropriate for black people to be accepted into white people's world. However, being on The Island, I have noticed that The New are freer with their looks; I see afros, wild and curly hair, that Diana Ross look, and the men with dreadlocks. The Established are more refined, well-groomed hair that is neat and is in place, and they are light-skinned. The New that looks like The Established looked like The Established but have The New's views. I shake my head at the concept of The New and The Established; money is green, and it spends the same way, quickly.

"I bet that be beautiful," LaKeya says, smiling.

I look at her, shocked at her compliment and her approval.

"Don't look at me like that," LaKeya said, smiling. She glances at me as she drives.

"I think you have great style!" LaKeya said. "Is it for me, no? I love how to incorporate the dreads with the classic look, urban chic."

I grin. I nod my head and look behind me at the pink elephant. She is still there winking at me. I roll my eyes and turn around. I know that I cannot go on as if nothing has happened. I cannot act like my oldest friend is not in trouble or in a situation that is not healthy. Her husband is a piece of –

"Journey," LaKeya says, calling me from my thoughts. "Talk to me about Nathan."

She has a big smile on her face. I don't want to discuss my relationship or pending relationship with Nathan. Although I am dying to share the escapade with a girlfriend, but LaKeya is not the girlfriend. Ironically we come to a red light; she looks at me, her eyes almond shape eyes smiling at me.

"I need to live vicariously through you." She says." "Talk to me! You told me that you weren't looking into dating anyone."

"It's nothing," I said with a grin. "We are enjoying each other's company."

She twisted her mouth and glared at me. That look means that she knows that there is something more, and she doesn't appreciate me being evasive. The light turns green, and she drives off.

"Are you being coy because of the past few days?" she asks.

I think about my answer. I can easily say no, but maybe a part of me doesn't want to tell her because I am still mad at her. She really didn't apologize to me or convey to me her issues. So why tell her that so far, the past few days, I had some much fun. Nathan has introduced me to some awesome people, and if she didn't have such a stick up her butt, we could have met Nathan's friends together, and they could possibly be new clients for Booker. I could tell her how great Nathan is in bed, and right now, we are just an Island Item with no promises, but I am enjoying this non-committed relationship. I am afraid to say yes, because it may stir up another argument and that pink elephant that sits in the back seat.

"No," I answer. "I just don't want to talk about Nathan. I am here with you. I don't want to discuss Booker or Nathan; it's a girl's day."

"Okay," LaKeya says, nodding her head.

She drives into a parking space, and together we get out and walk into Christina's Boutique.

We enter the boutique, and like before; I am amazed at how beautiful the ambiance is. The lavender-scented all-glass boutique is amazing.

"LaKeya, Journey," she said smiling, approaching us.

"Hi, Christina," LaKeya and I say together.

"You come back to see me," she smiles.

"Yes, I need a white gown," I reply.

"White?" Christina asks.

"Yes,"

"Come, follow me," Christina says.

128

"We follow Christina to that back mystery room that is all white that looks like a boutique in Heaven. Like before, there is a bottle of Champaign being chilled in a wine bucket. Christina's sales associates enter in pushing a rack of white gowns.

"Christina, do you have something with lavender, like jewelry or lace to go with these gowns?" LaKeya asks.

"Of course, darling," Christina says, smiling.

I sort through the rack of gowns trying to find something that does not make me look like a runaway bride. I want something that says Audrey, classic, yet I need that urban vibes that embrace my style. Christina must see that I am not happy with the selection that she provided; although her clothes are beautiful, elegant, and stylish, the selection that had been chosen are for brides, not upscale over the top christening ceremonies. Christina approaches me with a white lacy and silk jumpsuit. My mouth is agape. The breast, back, and crotch is white silk. Christina also brings lavender-colored diamond earrings.

"Yes," I said.

I take the outfit into the changing room and quickly change into this marvelous outfit.

I step out of the dressing room, and everyone in the room's mouths are agape. I smile at them and then stand in front of the mirror. The outfit looks amazing; it has a high lace collar, to my surprise, is not itchy or uncomfortable. The legs of the jumpsuit are wide leg, which I love and the sleeve are long, coming to my wrist. I smile and look to Christina.

"Yes," Christina says, smiling. "Very, very beautiful."

I nod my head smiling. I look to LaKeya she stands looking at me. I can see that she is not happy about my selection. She looks serious, waiting on her turn to criticize my outfit. I watch her take a deep breath, and she steps forward.

"You look beautiful, Journ." She says.

"Thank you," I say, still nervous, waiting for an explosion. "Did you select an outfit?"

"I had already found something." She informs.

"You know what I was thinking?" I begin. "Lavender corsages."

LaKeya smiles.

"That would be pretty," LaKeya says with a grin.

"So is it a go?" Christina asks?

"Yes!" I answer, "A big go!"

Everyone cheers, and we sip Champaign.

NEXT STOP IS THOM'S shoes. It seems like I am living a Deja Vu moment. LaKeya and I sit in the pretty chairs as Thom, as his girls Lady and Sandy, cater to us. We greet each other with kisses on both cheeks. Thom compliments how beautiful LaKeya and I look, and we tell him what we are looking for.

As Thom gets a few pairs of shoes for LaKeya and me, I hope that Thom will caress my feet, making me feel like a pampered goddess again, but then if he does and I like it, am I cheating on Nathan? Thom kneels down before me, and like a few days ago; he caresses my foot. I smile at him as we playfully flirt with each other. I giggle like a naughty school girl.

"Thom, you make me feel so sexy!" I say to him.

"You make me feel like man, enjoying my touch." He says back.

"I think I am going to throw up," LaKeya says, her mouth frowning and rolling her eyes.

"Here is something you can live vicariously with," I say to her and wink.

"Whatever Journ,"

Thom puts a pearl-colored platform five-inch heel on my foot. I know for a fact that these pair of shoes will look perfect for the christening. I nod my head, accepting the shoes as he puts the other pair of shoes on my feet. He helps me stand up, and I strut across the floor as if I am Naomi.

"Work it, baby," Thom says, and his girls cheer.

"Key?" I ask.

"Perfect," she says.

"We have a matching, pillbox style clutch," Lady said to me.

I nod my head, telling her yes to the shoes and the clutch. I look at LaKeya and walk back to the seats and sit next to her.

"You're turn." I say.

Thom takes LaKeya's foot and places a white leather pointy high heel shoe on her foot. She flexes her foot. She looks at me, and I shake my head.

"Too bridal," I say.

I slowly look around the showroom for something that will complement LaKeya's dress. From what she had explained to me, her dress is a beautiful white A-lined strapless stretch-Ponte shape. The pointy-type shoes would be perfect, but the whole white-on-white is too bridal.

"Key, get a pair of lavender Swarovski shoes," I suggest.

I hold up the pair of lavender shoes with Swarovski crystals that I was referring to. I hand them to Sandy so she can give them to Thom for LaKeya to try on. She tries them on. They look good on her feet.

"With lavender diamonds, this will be beautiful," I say, smiling.

LaKeya shrugs her shoulders.

"Swarovski is so low income." She comments.

"LaKeya, Swarovski covered shoes are not low income." I scoff. "No, it's not. If you get satin, you will look bridal and this is not a wedding. The Swarovski says we have money to burn."

LaKeya looks at Thom, and he nods his head agreeing with me.

"I think the round toe would be better," LaKeya said. "Do you have the round toe lavender Swarovski?"

"I have whatever you need baby." Thom said.

He snaps his fingers, and immediately, Lady appears with a box of Swarovski round-toe platform shoes. I am impressed. Where do they get these shoes?

She tries on the shoes, and Thom helps her stand. LaKeya walks back and forth in her shoes, and I must admit they are beautiful. I shake my head at the fact that these shoes are solely for her.

"Thom, I want a pair of these too," I said.

LaKeya looks at me; her eyes are intense.

"You're buying two pairs of shoes from here?" she asks.

"Technically, no, these will be my third pair," I said.

132

"How can you afford to pay for these shoes?" she asks.

"Are we doing this?" I question.

LaKeya takes in a deep breath. She closes her eyes.

"I'm sorry." She says. "Booker has me on a budget."

I nod my head, accepting her apology and her budget. Booker has her on a budget is laughable, unless she is an over spender, but I have never known LaKeya to spend foolishly.

"Thom, I will buy LaKeya's shoes," I say.

"Wait, what no!" LaKeya quickly declines.

"Call it a push gift for my godsons," I say with a wink.

"Journ," LaKeya begins to object, but she stops talking when she sees me shaking my head.

"Seriously, Key, I was not able to make the babies shower."

"A push gift is from your husband, not-,"

"A push gift is from whomever. Thom."

Thom nods his head, and within moments we are at the front so I can purchase the shoes. LaKeya walks out of the shop and gets smacked in the face by the bright sun.

"Food," I say, tilting my head back embracing the humidity.

We get in the car, and as LaKeya puts the key in the ignition, LaKeya looks at me.

"What?"

"You are rich." She asks rhetorically.

"Yes," I answer proudly.

LaKeya nods her head, accepting my response. It seems like she has now accepted my stance. She turns to face forward, facing the road. It seems as if there is a lot on her mind.

"I'm not rich." She says.

"Yes, you are," I reply.

"No, Booker is rich; I have no say to what is spent. You just brought, very, very expensive shoes, four pairs to be total, and you are not worried about moving money here to cover up."

I shake my head. She looks at me and shakes her head.

"I have done nothing with my life." She says.

I quickly look behind me to look at the pink elephant. She is still there, sitting in the back seat, looking at me. I take a deep breath. I am not sure how to move forward.

"What do you mean?" I ask.

"The past few days, I Googled you." She said. "I Googled my best friend, and so much came upon you. I saw YouTube videos of your speaking engagements and seminars. I saw YouTube videos of you talking to your fans about writing about building your business. I saw your website; plural. Journey, you have more than one website. You are a brand."

I never quite heard of me being a brand. I know that I work hard. I have people, marketing, and business managers that help me structure and plan my days so I can be current with videos and tutorials.

"My success came with hard work," I told her. "I remember my first book; I was sitting inside a bar and selling my book trying to make rent."

LaKeya looks at me, shocked at my confession.

"Now you are renting one of the most expensive lofts on The Island," LaKeya said coolly.

She looks off into the distance as if she is hypnotized. She looks at me and takes in a deep breath.

"I purposely suggested that loft because I didn't think you could afford it. I was so sure that coming to The Island was impossible for you, financially."

I just got forced fed a large pill, like a huge antibiotic. I suddenly flashed back to when I had a bad case of tonsillitis, and he gave me these horse pills to take. I had looked at him as if he was crazy. I have a sore throat, and you want me to swallow these large pills. LaKeya just told me something information that was hard to swallow. It's not even my pride that I have to swallow, just the idea that my friend, my sister, set me up to fail. I can't say anything. I don't know what to say.

"I want you to ask me to stay at the mansion," LaKeya said. "I wanted you to need me."

I look away, shaking my head and from the information that LaKeya told me.

"I'm sorry, Journ," LaKeya says. "I am very, very sorry. Like you said, we come from the pit, and now we are living the dream on The Island. You renting that loft is just one of the proof of your accomplishments. Me, birthing out two children for the sake of cementing myself into a family that I don't even like is proof of my accomplishment."

She is telling more information than a day of shopping.

"LaKeya, let's go back to the loft and talk, okay," I suggest.

I see tears well up in her eyes. She nods her head. She starts the car, and we ride off. We don't talk. I look in the back seat for the pink elephant, and she is still there. I shake my head, wondering when she is going to leave, but then again, we haven't really dealt with the issues; we just acknowledge them. I want so much for LaKeya to be happy in her life, even if it's with Booker, but she doesn't have to be with someone that she does not love for the sake of establishment or the sake of saying; "I'm married."

WE ARRIVE AT THE loft and quickly enter. I pray that Nathan is not here because this conversation is private and personal, and although his sister was hurt by Booker, Vision Campbell doesn't need any more validation. She goes into the Great Room, and I go into the kitchen to find some kind of junk food, but in my week of Mariah Carey whistle registry sex and Island Living, I have yet to stock the kitchen and refrigerator of cookies and ice cream. However, I see a full stock pantry.

"Nathan," I say.

I shake my head and smile. My Island Boyfriend is the best. I am going to miss this when the summer is over. I grab everything that my hands can carry and join LaKeya in the Great Room. She stands agape at me as I carry a load of food.

"What is this?" She asks.

"We need this. We are having a girlfriend moment."

I set everything down on the floor and then sit down in Indian style.

"I can't eat this," LaKeya says, sitting down on the floor with me.

"Yes, you can," I said, breaking open a bag of barbeque chips.

LaKeya opens up a bag of Oreos.

"So," I begin. "Talk to me."

LaKeya looks at me, her eyes soft. She is vulnerable.

"Well, as you know, I am unhappy." She confesses, shrugging her shoulders. "Booker makes me think that he has done me a favor."

I eat and listen.

"I don't come from a reputable family, per him. Although you and I both know that my folks are elegant and classy in their own right."

I nod my head.

"Yep," I said.

"Well," LaKeya said, biting an Oreo. "Per Booker's family, my family is not good enough. They are polyester and Cubic Zirconia, and we are silks and diamonds, but I want to be with them, especially the christening of the boys. I wish they were here now."

"So why put up with Booker and his family's stupidity?"

"Where else am I going to go? If Booker decides to leave me in our world, I will look like a loser. I don't come from a pedigree like his."

"But if you leave him, you are showing that world that you don't need Booker Matthews," I said. "Key, you have a Sociology Degree; you can help women who are in bad relationships get out and find their self-worth."

She looks away.

"Wine!" I said.

Quickly I walk into the kitchen and get the bottle of wine that Nathan had a place in the refrigerator. I quickly uncork it and grab two wine glasses and run back into the Great Room. I sit down and pour us each a glass of wine.

"Journey, we are going to get sick eating all this junk food and drinking."

"So what," I said. "We are on vacation; we can puke our brains out and sleep the whole day," I said, sipping my wine.

"I won't get any alimony if I leave Booker." She said. "And the boys, well, his family can fight me for full custody."

"I'll take care of you," I said. "You and the boys. You can stay with me in New York, and I'll take care of you, help you get back on your feet."

"Why would you do that?" she asks.

"Because," I said, shoving a handful of chips in my mouth. "You're my best friend."

LaKeya shakes her head at the idea that I would take care of her. I look at her, nodding my head, which tells her that I will take care of her. I sip my wine to wash down the chips, hit my chest to let out a belch.

"I don't know Journey," LaKeya said. "I can't let you do this. It's appreciated, but I have to figure something out."

"You can't stay in a toxic relationship," I said to her. "It will kill you."

"Kill me?" she asks.

"Yes, the men that I dated, they were toxic. I didn't know my left hand from my right. I didn't know if I was coming or going with regards to the relationship. If Booker can see the type of woman you really are, then he won't care what his parents thought. He would defend you to his parents and tell them to kiss his-,"

"Okay, Journey, I get it," LaKeya said.

I take in a deep breath and try to escape the nausea I am beginning to feel from consuming so much junk food and wine so fast. I run my tongue along my teeth.

"We were not raised with the determination of greatness to be belittled or demeaned." I said, "Our parents wanted more from us. They wanted us to control the atmosphere in our lives, not the atmosphere controls us."

"How do you control the atmosphere?" LaKeya asks as if my statement is crazy.

"My ex-boyfriend has been calling me nonstop since I found out that he is engaged to another pretty light-skinned woman. I don't and won't answer the phone because I control how I am treated."

LaKeya shakes her head.

"I don't punch in and out of work; I have people working for me."

LaKeya nods her head understanding me.

"I have worked for years to get to this level. Your malicious attempt to make me need you backfired in your pretty little face."

"Journey, I said I was sorry." LaKeya defends herself.

"I forgive you," I said, smiling. "But never plot against another queen."

I finish my glass of wine as LaKeya looks at the clock.

"I better get back." She says.

"Okay," I said.

Together we walk to the front door. I give her a big and tight hug. I watch her leave and get into her car. She puts on her seat belt, and she waves at me. I wave back, and she drives off.

I notice the wind starting to blow, blowing hot, humid air making the trees sway. I saw clouds starting to form. The sky is not white but now a haunting dark gray. It looks like rain. As beautiful as I think the rain is, I have a feeling that something strange is going on. I hope LaKeya gets home safely and hope Nathan is safe where ever he is. I quickly shut the door and go inside.

I return to the Great Room and sigh at the mess we, I, made. I begin to clean up, put the chips and cookies away and the empty bags away. I pour myself a glass of wine and sit in the Great Room with the lights out, listening to the rain fall.

The sky is now dark, and the rain violently hits the windows. I think about this afternoon, LaKeya confessing to me what she had done. I would never do one of my girlfriends like that to set them up to fail. I encourage, applauded, and support. I think of my girlfriends back home. If I were to tell about LaKeya's attempt, they would make me end my friendship with her. They would tell me that we have outgrown each other and convince me that it's okay to never speak with her again. My thoughts would be on the boys. They tell me not my problem and let Booker's boujee family to take care of the boys and that I should write about her stuck-up mentality in my next book. I chuckle at my friends in New York. They are tough but loving. I don't remember having to validate myself with them. Any new accomplishment they have been there to celebrate with me.

I shake my head. None of these really matters. I know who I am. I know what I worked for and how hard I worked. She is confessing that she tried to set me up, but I fell into her trap. I brought clothes and shoes that I don't need. Although I can afford them, it's the point. I needed to prove my worth and my value. I did that with Marcus and I did that with LaKeya. Will I ever be at the place in my life where I don't have to prove myself worthy to anyone? I can walk into a room of millionaires and billionaires and know that I know, that I know that I belong here. I can toast my Champaign with them, and we laugh at life, not old money or new money, not light-skinned or dark skin.

THE STORM IS VICIOUS; the winds blow hard and violently shake the trees and rattles the windows of the loft. I haven't heard from Nathan. As I look out the window and see the storm, I close my eyes and pray and hope that Nathan is all right. I notice that the lights begin to flicker. Quickly, I move through the loft to find candles, matches or lighters, and a flashlight. I find them and place the candles in the Great Room, the bathroom, and the bedroom. I walk around the Great Room thinking, besides the television on to some re-run and the sound of the storm, it's quiet, a perfect time to write.

Writing is my therapy. Sometimes I feel purged after writing rather I am writing in my journal or writing a fiction novel. Within the past few days, I have experienced a lot; I'm almost nervous as to what will happen in the next few months. I know that I cannot go through my summer trying to validate myself. I want to spend these next few months writing, doing vacation things, snorkeling, zip-lining, water skiing, parasailing, or hiking. I am not the outdoors type, but I need to do something other than to validate my worth to The Established.

I walk into the bedroom, and grab my journal and pen from one of my travel bags and begin to jot down a fe ideas. I want to write something epic; I would defiantly write about the experience I had this past week. Of course, I would change the names and create a twist. Writing is a gift that I am both thankful for and sensitive about. When I was a little girl, I knew that I wanted to write because my parents would always find me staring at the clouds. I would make up these stories about the clouds. My parents would say:

"You have an active imagination."

I knew at that moment; I wanted to be a writer. My parents always encouraged my writing. I had a knack for creative writing. Considering that being successful as a writer can be financially difficult, my parents also encouraged me to have a Plan B. They never discouraged me from going for my dreams but to be mindful. So I learned the business of writing, marketing, and promoting.

The storm continues to rein havoc on The Island; I continue to write. I write about the beauty of The Island, from the cloudless skies and the diamond-colored sand. The people black people, the light-skinned, brown-skinned, and the dark-skinned. I write about The New and The Established. I write about best friends and new friends.

THE KNOCK AT THE is alarming because from where I come from, that pounding was from the police, or there is an emergency. As the pounding persists, I race to the front door, and Nathan is standing on the other side. I open the door; he is soaking wet.

"Nathan!" I exclaim.

He steps in but only into the foyer. He is breathing hard. I can see that something is wrong, very wrong.

"What's wrong?"

"LaKeya and Booker."

I hold my breath.

"What?" I ask.

"He's dead." Nathan answers.

I gasp.

I DON'T REMEMBER PUTTING my shoes on. I don't remember getting into the car. Nathan races through the streets on The Island.

"What happened?" I ask. "We were together this afternoon."

"I am not sure; one of the servants called me to come over. They had said that LaKeya and Booker were arguing. There was a shooting, and Booker fell off the balcony."

"Oh my goodness!" I exclaimed, covering my face. "What happened?"

WE ARRIVE AT THE mansion. Ironically the rain has stopped. However, the humidity has broken, and it's a bit cool outside. The Island Patrol and the coroner are here. I see servants talking with the police. I see the coroner brings Booker's body on the stretcher, my knees buckled. Nathan quickly grabs me. He is covered up. I see them put Booker in the coroner's van, and within minutes the van drives away, revealing LaKeya. She is standing still, covered in a blanket.

"KEY!" I exclaim.

Quickly, Nathan and I race to her. I reach her first and hug her; tight, and then Nathan hugs her.

"What-what?" I said, trying to talk.

I look up and see The Island Patrol walking Monica to their car; she is wearing handcuffs. My eyes grow to the size of quarters. I look at LaKeya.

"What happened?" I ask.

"When I came back from our afternoon, I found Booker cheated on me with her."

I cover my mouth, shocked, appalled, and disgusted by the idea. I frowned my face.

"How is she even his type?" I question.

Suddenly one of The Island Patrol approaches LaKeya. He looks at us and acknowledges us with a nod of his head.

"Mrs. Matthews, you are free to go, but please be available for questions." He said.

"Yes."

The Island Patrol leaves, and LaKeya looks at me with tears in her eyes. She takes a deep breath as the tears fall down upon her cheek.

"Journey, I can't stay in that house. Can the boys-,"

I quickly take her hands.

"You don't have to ask," I said, shaking my head. "Let's grab you a few things, get the boys and go back to the loft."

Quickly, LaKeya and I packed clothes for herself and the boys. We pack their formula, their car seats. Nathan helped take down their play pins, and he packed them in his car. LaKeya told the staff that they are dismissed for the remainder of the summer. As we begin to walk to Nathan's care, I noticed that she takes a final look. She lets out a sigh, and tears fall from her eyes.

"It's going to be okay, Key," I say to her.

She looks at me and shakes her head. Her nose is red, and she is bleary-eyed. She looks so tired and frail.

With the boys and LaKeya in the back seat, me in the passenger seat, we ride off to my loft. So many questions go through my mind.

What happened? Is my biggest question.
Booker is dead?
And there is the most horrifying question:
Monica?
That question makes me want to vomit.

THE BABIES SLEEP SOUNDLY, in the guest room that LaKeya has taken for herself and her boys. I watch as she lays receiving blankets over them. I like watching her with her boys. She is gentle and nurturing. As she looks up, I smile at her. I nod my head, in a sense telling her that everything is going to be all right.

"Come into the Great Room," I say.

LaKeya grabs the baby monitor and follows me into the Great Room. To our surprise, Nathan had prepared cold-cut sandwiches, and there is a bottle of wine chilling. Everything is laid out on the floor like a picnic, with a blanket and a few throw pillows. The lights are turned off and the television is not on, just the candles that had been burning before Nathan had come to the house.

"You have to be hungry," Nathan said to LaKeya.

She shrugs her shoulders, and together we all sit on the floor. LaKeya doesn't move or attempt to fix herself anything to eat. I shot Nathan and look, and he shrugs. Quickly, I grab a plate and put a sandwich on her plate. As I am doing this, Nathan pours LaKeya a glass of wine. We set both the plate and wine glass in front of her. She looks at us. Through candlelight, she looks so helpless. She looks off into the distance. Nathan and I wait for her to either come back mentally or for her to eat. She shakes her head as tears fall down from her eyes.

"I caught him in the very act." She says coolly. "I came home. I had hoped to take a quick nap. I go towards the master bedroom and hear noises. I think to myself: 'Are the servants having sex in my room?' I burst into the bedroom and see Booker and Monica going at it! They jump and scurry, trying to get dressed, and Booker tried to lie. I start screaming at him and at her."

"What about the staff?" I ask.

"They knew what was going on. Not one of them tried to warm me," she answers. "You know what gets to me? None of them, not one treated me with respect. I am the lady of the house, and they didn't jump when I said so, only when Booker said so. Booker pays them, so they kept his secret."

"Key, Monica is ratchet. You have to know that she had no class."

"Monica and Booker had been childhood friends. Their parents swore to me that nothing has ever happened with them." LaKeya says, shaking her head. "I asked him, how could he in our house, in our bed, with our babies in the adjoining room? I started punching him. I started throwing things. I ran into the bedroom to start packing my bags. Booker ran after me trying to stop me. I can't understand why he doesn't want me; he doesn't need me. We fought in the bedroom. I tried to pack the boys' things. Next thing you know, I hear, 'Tell her Booker!', it was Monica, standing in the doorway taunting me. I snap. I started fighting her. I fought hard. I punched, kicked, clawed. I beat her down until I thought she blacked out. I screamed at Booker. I am a mother; I don't fight. I don't beat down women."

LaKeya shakes her head.

"I yelled to the servants to call Nathan! The one time they actually listened to me. I remove myself from the bedroom, Booker follows me. Now we are in the sitting room. The suddenly, Monica emerges. She had a gun."

I gaps and cover my mouth.

"Yes, she tried to shoot me!" LaKeya exclaims. "She is shooting, and Booker and I are ducking and hiding for cover; bullets are flying everywhere. He manages to grab her and knocked her down again. He manages to get the gun out of her hands, and they wrestle and fight. They fight out of the sitting room and into the balcony; before you knew it, she manages to give him one good push. The banister of the balcony must have been loose because it broke, and Booker-,"

"Say no more," I said, shaking my head.

I take her hands into mine. She puts her head down and sobs softly. I feel tears hit my hands. I didn't realize that I had been crying. As she cries, I put my arms around her, and we sob softly together. I have no words for what she is going through.

"I had my suspicions that he had been cheating on me. Thought he be decent enough not to do it in our home. I thought it was Vision Campbell."

I look at Nathan.

"Why would you think that?" Nathan asks.

"I know that she is your sister," LaKeya says. "I know about Booker and her love affair before me. However, I know that she was the one he loved."

"My sister wouldn't sleep with another woman's husband." Nathan coolly defends.

"No, she just makes her image seen all over The Island." LaKeya snaps.

"Key," I admonish softly as I gently rub her hands.

"What my sister does to promote herself and what your husband did is very different." Nathan defends.

"Nathan," I admonish. "Both of you, snapping at each other is not going to fix anything."

A moment passes before anyone speaks.

"I'm sorry," LaKeya says. "It's hard to live up to her shadow."

I can tell that Nathan understands LaKeya's point, but he chooses to say nothing. LaKeya lets out a sigh.

"I have to tell his family that their golden child is dead," LaKeya says, shaking her head. "I have to bury a man that disrespected me on all levels."

"I'll be here, Key; you don't have to do it alone," I said to her.

"They are going to try to take my boys from me," LaKeya says as tears fill her eyes.

She shakes her head and covers her face.

"They can do that. They do evil and malicious things like that!"

"They won't" I said.

"Journey, you can't help me. You don't have as much money as they do; I know you don't." she wept.

"Key, I got you!" I said, crying.

I take her hands into my hands and kiss them. I am weeping.

"It's going to be okay," I said, crying. "I promise you. I won't let anything happen to the boys. I will take care of you."

"I don't want to bury him." She says, "Let his family deal with it."

"Key, you-,"

"No, Journ, I am not doing anything for him. I birthed two babies at the same time for that man. I shunned

148

my family for him, and he treated me like a dog, less than a dog."

I close my eyes. The strain in her voice is breaking my heart. I have never seen her so weak ever in my life. I don't know how to comfort her if I can comfort her. I look at Nathan; he turns his head. This is breaking his heart too.

"Key, drink; it may relax you," I say, handing her the glass of wine. "Come, baby, drink."

Reluctantly, LaKeya takes the glass and drinks the wine. I nod my head approvingly.

"What did the policemen say?" Nathan asks.

"The servants all vouched for me," LaKeya answered. "Told the patrol everything that happened. Found out that Monica has some illegal dealings. They are shipping her back to the States."

I sit shock but not shocked by the fact that Monica is a shaky character.

"Journ, I am so sorry for everything," LaKeya says, crying.

"Stop, stop, it's okay," I said, comforting. "Key, eat something, baby, please."

"I'm not hungry." She says.

"You have to eat, please." I almost beg.

LaKeya shakes her head. I take in a deep breath.

"Let's get you to bed," I suggest.

"I can't sleep," she says, shaking her head.

"I'll stay with you until you fall asleep," I suggest.

I stand up and hold out my hand to her. Reluctantly she takes my hand and stands. I lead her to the guest room. The babies are still sleeping soundly. Together we sit on the bed. I take a pillow and place it on my lap. She lays her head on my lap, and I caress the side of her face.

I shake my head. How did she get to this place? Why does this have to be her life? This is not what her parents signed her up for. I close my eyes and the idea of telling them everything. I can see the horrifying look on their faces. I can see the pain in their eyes, and LaKeya has to face Booker's family regarding the boys. She is entitled to every dime as his widow. I know they will fight her. She is not prepared to fight. I take in a deep breath, realizing that I am going to have to fight for her. I can fight. I will fight.

SHE IS FINALLY SLEEPING soundly. I slowly slip out from under LaKeya and go into The Great Room to find Nathan now sitting on the couch. He had cleaned up the little picnic. I sit next to him on the couch. He places his hand on my thigh.

"This is a mess," I said.

"It's more than a mess," Nathan said. "You must be exhausted."

I shake my head, but I am tired. Today has been a draining day.

"Thank you for staying," I said.

"Of course." He said, "Booker Matthews is a piece of work."

"Is his family really monsters?" I ask.

"Just say they have money to buy, resell and buy again," Nathan said.

"Will they take her babies?" I ask.

"They can," Nathan said.

"LaKeya has a fight on her hands," I said.

Nathan lifts his arms so he can put his arms around me. I lay my head on his chest and fall asleep.

I DON'T REMEMBER SLEEPING, but I wake up to the sound of crying babies and the sunlight in my eyes. I sit up and look at the clock, and it reads a little after ten a.m. I run into the bathroom to take a shower. After my shower, I quickly get dressed and join my guest in the kitchen. There is already a display of food, waffles and fruit, eggs, bacon, and sausage. There is also a fresh pot of coffee. I look at Nathan, and he smiles. He is holding a baby, and LaKeya is holding another. LaKeya is feeding the one baby with the bottle while Nathan gently bounces the other baby and takes them to the window to look at the scenery. How did he manage to cook everything with LaKeya and the boys here?

"I'm sorry, I slept so late," I said.

"No apologies needed," LaKeya said with a grin.

"How are you feeling?" I ask.

"The fact that I am a widow and sleeping in my best friend's rented loft, I'm doing well."

I shake my head at her sadistic comment. I have a feeling that she will be a bit cynical and sadistic more than the next few days but the next few years.

"I made some phone calls," Nathan informs us.

I sip my coffee and look at Nathan; he continues:

"I know a few powerhouse lawyers that can help you, LaKeya in the event that Booker's family tries to get unethical."

"Unethical?" she questions, the word Nathan used.

Nathan shrugs his shoulders.

"I don't have any money! Once Booker's family finds out what happens, they will cut me off." LaKeya expresses.

"I can cover it," I said to her. "I told you, I can help."

The baby that she is holding stops drinking. She sets the bottle down on the table, puts the baby against her shoulder, and lightly tabs his back to burp him. I smile at his little head, looking around, trying to see his surroundings.

"Which one is he?" I ask, feeling embarrassed.

"David," LaKeya answers me. "I still have to mark them some kind of way to tell them apart. You know Booker's parents fought me on naming him David because of David and Bathsheba, never mind, David and Goliath. Condemn the great king, excuse Booker for his nonsense. I am going to raise my boys better."

"You will." I encourage. "David and Isaiah, great men in the Bible."

LaKeya continues to tap lightly on David's back. She looks up at Nathan.

"You're named after a great man of God too, Nathaniel."

Nathan nods his head and shrugs his shoulders modestly.

"Doesn't mean I am a great man. Just have a big reputation to live up to." He says.

"Why are you being so nice to me?" She asks. "You are Booker's friend."

Nathan takes in a deep breath and then looks at LaKeya.

"I saw what he put my sister through," Nathan said. "She was a mess. Worse than what her ex-husband put her through."

"What did he do?" LaKeya asks.

"Made her feel that she will never measure up. My sister had good credit, no criminal background, was an upstanding citizen. She said her pleases and thank you; the may I's. But per Booker's family, she is nothing because of her background. My parents raised her; that means that even though she was born into rejection, my family loved and raised her as their own. So does that mean that my family is not good enough?"

I shake my head at the hatred and bigotry that some people have. What difference does it make of someone's background? Dr. King said it should base on their character, not color. However, with Booker's family, color meant nothing, a character meant nothing, it was their background, and if their background is not suitable enough then-oh well; too bad. Nathan's response is the confirmation that I need that the dream I had the other day is true. He helped Vision Campbell to be the force that she needed to be to get revenge on The Established people that spurned her and Booker.

With David still in her arms, she stands up and slowly paces the kitchen. She continues to pat his back.

"Come on, Lil Man, burp." She encourages softly.

"Key, when are your parents coming?" I ask.

"This evening," LaKeya answers.

"I can pick them up at the airport and bring them here." I offered.

"Thanks," she replies.

"Booker's parents still need to be notified." She says.

"I know," I said. "How are we going to tell them?"

LaKeya shrugs, and then baby burps. She looks at him, and she smiles.

"I should start making phone calls and telling everyone that instead of the christening, there will be a funeral," LaKeya said.

"I'll help you," I suggest.

I take in a deep breath as I think about all that needs to be done, informing everyone that Booker Matthews is now dead.

WE SIT IN THE in the office of the loft. We have booze and tissue. Vision's office is beautiful. The desk is made of red cedar wood; there is a computer, printer, fax machine. There is a bookshelf with a few books and magazines; business magazine and fashion magazine. There is a cream-colored love seat and recliner chair in the office, and a large flat-screen television is mounted on the wall and a bay window with a beautiful view of the scenery. When I first entered the office a few days ago, I shook my head at the beauty of this room. Who needs this much splendor in the office. There is a crystal glass that held pretty ink pens, those fancy pens that cost a hundred dollars per pen.

I sit in the love seat next to her as she takes her cell phone and begins to make her phone calls. The first call is to Booker's parents. I watch her handshake as she goes into her contacts and searches for BOOKER'S PARENTS; she taps their names, and the phone rings. Tears form in her eyes, and she takes in a deep breath. She sets the phone on speaker.

"Hello," said the voice on the other end.

"Hi, it's Keya. Can I speak to Mr. and Mrs. Matthews?" LaKeya says.

"Just a moment, please."

The silence in the office is loud and threatening. I look out the bay window and don't see any candy-colored birds flying. Instead, the sun is bright, as if there was no storm last night. It's as if Vision has fairies come and clean up the debris from the storm and made The Island beautiful again.

"Yes," said the voice on the phone, it's a woman.

"Hi, Mrs. Booker, it's Keya." She says nervously.

"Yes," the woman says, coolly.

"Ah, I have some disturbing news to tell you." LaKeya begins.

"What," Mrs. Booker said.

I shake my head at how short and cold she is to the woman that birthed her grandchildren.

"Booker," LaKeya says, starting to cry.

Her voice shakes as she said his name.

"Booker has died," LaKeya says, crying.

I shake my head. Butterflies flutter rapidly in my stomach. I pour myself and LaKeya a drink, and I swallow mine.

"What?!" Mrs. Matthews asks.

I can hear the confusion in her voice.

"Who is this?" Mrs. Matthews asks.

"It's Keya," LaKeya says, sniffing. "Booker has died."

"Clarence!" she screams, "Clarence!"

LaKeya covers her face and sobs. I wrap the tears from my eyes.

"Give me the phone," I said, taking the phone from LaKeya.

"Mrs. Matthews," I said. "Mrs. Matthews."

"They killed Booker!" I hear her scream.

"Hello," someone on the other end says. "This is Lee, their head butler."

"Lee, this is Journey, LaKeya's friend. "I introduce myself."

"What is going on?" Lee asks.

I let out a sigh.

"Booker died last night," I said.

"Oh my goodness, what happened?" Lee asked.

"He fell off the balcony," I said, smiling.

"Oh my goodness," Lee gasps.

I hear some someone grab the phone.

"Hello, hello, this is Clarence Matthews," said Booker's father. "What in God's name is going on?"

The idea of making this announcement again is killing me. I look at LaKeya, and she is still crying, sobbing.

"Mr. Matthews," I said. "My name is Journey; I'm a friend of LaKeya's. Booker-,"

"What happened?!" he exclaims. "What have you done to my son?"

"Your son fell off a balcony. Please come to The Island." I said.

"Where is LaKeya?" Mr. Matthews questions.

"I'm here, sir," LaKeya says, crying.

"What did you do?" Mr. Matthews asks.

She shakes her head.

"Your son cheated on me, and his *mistress* pushed him off the balcony." LaKeya hissed.

The pain in her voice hits me in the throat. I try to clear my throat, but it feels like it's a lump. I hear a lot of commotion in the background, people talking, and Mrs. Matthews screaming. The sound of LaKeya's and her cry will haunt me forever.

"Come to The Island, please." I request.

"Hello, Journey." Said another voice; I assume it is Lee. "I will make arrangements for Mr. and Mrs. Matthews to come to The Island."

"Okay," I said.

"Can I call you?" Lee asks.

"Yes, of course." I reply. "here is my number; please let me know when you're ready."

I give Lee my phone number.

"Thank you." He says and then hangs up the phone.

I let out a sigh. My body feels as if it has done a hardcore cardio workout. LaKeya sits on the love seat, staring off in the distance. Her eyes are red from crying so hard. My eyes are wet themselves from crying. Nathan walks into the office. I look up at him. He has a look on his face as if he is nervous but not nervous. Then suddenly I notice a shadow behind him. Nathan steps aside, and stepping forward is Vision Campbell.

I gasp. I stand up as if royalty has now entered the room. I look at LaKeya and rigorously snap at her, trying to pull her from her trance. LaKeya looks at me; I tilt my head at our visitor.

She looks at Vision, just as stunned as I am, and quickly she stands up.

"Ms. Campbell," I say, holding my breath.

She is as beautiful in person as she is in the photos of her. She stands before us wearing all black, a black pair of wide-leg slacks with a black off-the-shoulder boat neck, long-sleeved style top. She wears her dreadlocks in a messy bun high on the top of her head and large emerald-cut diamond earrings. Her hazel-colored eyes look like citrine diamonds. I can't help but stare at her and fight the urge to drool.

"Ha-ha, hello." I stammer.

I glance at Nathan and then return to staring at Vision Campbell.

"Hello," her voice is soft.

Her eyes look to LaKeya. She looks at her with a soft and gentle look. LaKeya looks at me.

"Hello," LaKeya says.

"Hello," she says to LaKeya. "My name is Vision."

Vision introduces herself and approaches us. She extends her hand for us to shake. Nervously, I shake her soft hand, and then LaKeya shakes her hand.

"I am told there has been some trouble." Vision says.

Like how Nathan used the word unethical, Vision uses the word trouble. She looks at LaKeya with gentle and trusting eyes.

"I'm here to help."

LaKeya passes out and falls to the ground.

Nathan and I quickly move to get her to the love seat. I watch Vision leave the room, and she quickly returns with a warm cloth to place on her head.

"Key," I said, softly tapping her face. "Key, come on, baby."

She moans softly.

"Here she comes," I said, smiling. "Come on, mamas. Come on."

"What-what happens?" she says.

I watch her opens her eyes, and she looks at the loving sunrise in the office. She closes her eyes again, because like anyone that looks directly at the sun, they have to shield their eyes, and that is the same for looking directly at Vision Campbell.

Slowly LaKeya tries to sit up.

"I'm sorry," LaKeya apologizes.

"It's okay," we all say to her.

"I hear you had quite an ordeal." Vision says.

Ordeal, again, a common word that is used to relate to a heavy issue. I quickly look around to see if there is a pink elephant in the room; there is none.

"We just talked with Booker's parents," I said. "Their butler Lee is preparing for them to come."

Nathan nods his head, accepting my report.

"How can I help you?" Vision asks, LaKeya.

"Why would you help me?" LaKeya asks. "You don't know me."

"I know the issue all too well." She says softly. "His family will not bully you. I will see to that."

"Why are you willing to help me?" LaKeya asks tears form in her eyes.

"Because I know the pain that you're in, and I vowed to never let another woman suffer from the hands or mind of the Matthews Family."

"Yes, but would flaunt your beauty so Booker can see you," LaKeya says.

Vision Campbell doesn't justify her method of revenge to LaKeya. The babies start to cry. LaKeya stands and leaves the room to see about them.

"You want help?" I ask.

"No, they just need changed." She answers.

Together, the three of us, stand still looking at each other. I am at a loss for words. What does one say to the most beautiful woman in the world? She looks at me. I smile nervously.

"Let's go into the Great Room," Nathan suggests.

Together the three of us walk into the Great Room. I watch Vision sit down on the couch. She moves like a swan. Nathan sits down beside her, and I sit across from them on the love seat.

"My brother has told me a lot about you." Vision says, smiling.

I almost want to squint from the shine behind her smile; even her smile is beautiful. I do squint my eyes and shield my eyes, blaming it on the sun shining through the window.

"I also follow you on Instagram. I am impressed with your work." Vision said.

Vision Campbell impressed with me? I say to myself.

"I also have read your work." Vision said, smiling. "I enjoy your books."

Now I want to pass out. I have no clue what to say to her. Saying thank you is too mild and so basic, but compared to her, I am basic.

"Thank you," I say humbly.

Vision looks at Nathan and smiles at her.

"Your home is beautiful, Ms. Campbell," I said.

"Please, call me Vision." She says.

I smiled at her. I take in a deep breath and focus on the issue at hand.

"What are you going to do for Keya?" I ask.

"For starters, we are going to make sure that the Matthews don't get custody of her babies." Vision says to me. "Second, I have a team of lawyers and investigators who have been keeping a close eye on Booker Matthews and his family and their bank, and there have been a lot of illegal dealings. So if and when they try it with LaKeya, we'll be ready."

LaKeya enters the Great Room. She sits next to me.

"I was just telling Journey that I have a team of lawyers and investigators that have been watching The

160

Matthews and the bank, and there have been a lot of illegal dealings."

LaKeya eyes widen to the size of quarters. She quickly looks at me and then covers her mouth.

"My team will make sure that you keep those beautiful babies and collect royally as Booker's widow."

"I can't pay for this," LaKeya said, tears falling down her eyes.

Like a swan, Vision stands up and slowly walks to LaKeya. She kneels down before her and takes LaKeya's hands. Vision Campbell is humble.

"You don't need money with me, just your friendship."

LaKeya nods her head and lets out a sigh. I can feel that there has been a weight lifted off her should. Vision walks back to the couch and sits next to her brother.

"What time are Booker's parents scheduled to arrive?" Vision asks.

"I literally just got off the phone with them when you arrived," I informed. "Their butler is to call me with any updates."

"What about your family, LaKeya?"

"My parents are due to arrive in the evening. LaKeya answers. "I still need to notify the guest, the caterer, the flowers."

"I will handle that." Vision volunteers. "Give me the list of names, and I will cancel everything."

"Everything is at the mansion," LaKeya said.

"That is okay; I will have my people pick it up." Vision said. "I want you to get some rest."

"I'm not tired," LaKeya said.

"It's okay," Vision said. "Get some rest."

LaKeya looks at me. I nod my head, agreeing with Vision. Reluctantly LaKeya stands up and walks to the guest room.

AN HOUR HAS PASSED. No one has really said anything. LaKeya and the boys sleep soundly in the guest room. I hear Vision sitting in the breakfast nook on her phone. To my assumption, she is making the phone calls to her people regarding getting the list of names to cancel the christening.

Nathan has been sitting on the couch in the Great Room watching ESPN. Lee, the Matthews' head butler, called me to inform me that they are on their private jet on their way to The Island, and it should landing tomorrow morning. I gave him the address to the loft so the Matthews will know where to come to.

I walk into the kitchen to prepare food. I don't know what I am going to cook, but food is in order. I see salmon in the refrigerator, as well as plenty of vegetables.

Did Nathan get salmon? I ask myself.

I decided to barbeque, grilled salmon, and grilled vegetables on a kabob sound good. There is plenty of wine, so I put a few bottles in the refrigerator to chill, and I prepare the food.

"Can I help you with anything?" I hear.

I turn around to see Vision Campbell standing in the kitchen. I smile at her. She slowly approaches me, and I hand her a few vegetables to chop up for the kabobs. I season the salmon with Old Bay seasoning and lemon pepper.

"You don't know what a lifesaver you are, Vision," I said.

She smiles bashfully.

"One thing I learned is to always be prepared." Vision said. "I learned the hard way from my first marriage. If it wasn't for my brother, I probably would be dead. LaKeya is lucky to have a friend like you."

"Thank you," I reply.

I look at her trying to believe that someone this beautiful is human, but as I season the salmon, I look at the real, live person that has commanding and demanding beauty. I take in a deep breath.

"You seem to be doing well for yourself," Vision said. "I followed your career. I am impressed and proud of the life that you made."

I look at her shocked by her admiration.

"What?" she asks. "Can't another woman, black woman that is, applaud and compliment another queen. And yes, I said black. With that one drop rule, I am a black woman."

"I didn't mean anything on those lines," I said to her. "I am just shocked at how down to earth you are. You look like heaven, and yet you are so normal."

"Normal," she chuckles, sliding the vegetables on the kabobs. "There is more normal to me than one chooses to believe. Present company excluded."

"Not offended," I said with a grin.

She smiles back.

"My brother has spoken very highly of you." She says. "He told me you are a big seafood lover, so I brought in the salmon here."

"Your brother is a nice guy; he seems to always know what to do," I said. "I am glad that we have gotten to know each other."

"I hope that once all this has ugliness is over; we can be friends." She says.

"I like that," I said, smiling at her. "May I ask you a question?"

"Sure." She answers.

"Are you really very reclusive?" I ask.

"When you look like me, you have to be aware of your surroundings plus, with my businesses, I don't have time to socialize as much."

"Businesses, haunting Booker?" I ask.

"No, I actually have legitimate businesses. I own property, banks, this Island."

I nod my head.

"When Nathan told me that you owned this Island, I must say that I was impressed on how you overcame your obstacles to own an Island."

Vision smiles.

"It really isn't that hard." She says to me. "Plowing the land, making roads and streets, the beaches, was hard."

"People can live here forever, and you be rich," I comment.

She shrugs her shoulders.

"People can move somewhere else, and I lose money." Vision says. "Don't look at the glamour, but at the background. The glamour is just the smoke; when the smoke fades, what do you have, all due respects to your friend, a mess."

I take in a deep breath. She has made a very valid point. Together we go on to the patio and lit up the grill. As I prepare the charcoal and then pour fire fluid on them, I think about what Vision just told me: to not focus on the glamour. I know that my life, although not focused on being glamorous, I focused on how to make it seem amazing. My dating life, dating the pretty boy or the handsome one, only got my feelings hurt. Being that girl to

164

my man, so I look glamorous to him. Me trying to validate myself to LaKeya, although now I know it was pointless, was to appear glamorous because I, me, an old friend from the hood, has made it.

"Vision, if we should not focus on the glamour, then why this beautiful island?" I ask, laying the salmon on the grill.

"There is nothing wrong with liking beautiful things, but don't let that be your motivating source of power."

"Then explain why you chose to haunt Booker," I said.

"Because his family chose not to choose me, and they are so vain and arrogant that they fail to realize that they chose me every time they set foot on this island."

I look at my watch and realize that it's about time to get LaKeya's parents from the airport.

"I can send for a car to get them." Vision suggests.

"That be nice," I said.

She grabs her cell phone from her back pocket and what I assume, sends a text to her minions. She looks at me and grins.

"I need to get me a few of those," I said.

"What?" she asks.

"Minions," I reply.

She laughs at my joke.

LAKEYA WAITS NERVOUSLY FOR, her parents to get out of the car and walk to the loft. She nervously cracks her knuckles and bites her pretty manicured nails as she paces in the Great Room. Vision Campbell and I sit in the Great Room with LaKeya. The babies are in the Guess

Room, dress and ready to meet to Grandma and Grandpa Wilson.

"Key, relax," I say to her.

"Are her parents anything like Booker's?" Vision asks me.

"God no," LaKeya answers, shaking her head. "I guess I don't want to cry again." Vision nods her head.

The doorbell rings. LaKeya stops pacing. I stand up and walk to the front door. I answer it. Standing in front of me is Miss. Donna and Mr. Jake!"

"Journey!" They exclaim.

We give each other a big tight hug.

"You are looking good, girl!" Miss Donna says, smiling.

"Trying to keep up with you, Diva!" I exclaim.

"Hush," Miss Donna smiles bashfully.

She is still a beauty. LaKeya is a splinting image of her mother. Miss Donna wears her hair in small pixie cute, and she wears pearl earrings and a soft pink dress, and white sandals. Mr. Jake has a full beard that is now gray, and his head is shaven bald. He looks good, wearing a light blue Polo shirt and a pair of Khaki pants, and dark brown loafers.

I take them both by the hands and lead them to the Great Room.

"Hi, Mom, Daddy." LaKeya smiles nervously.

She approaches them, and they embrace. LaKeya begins to cry as she hugs her parents. I see Miss Donna crying.

"What's the matter?" Miss. Donna asks.

"Where is Booker?" Mr. Jake asks.

"Um," LaKeya hesitates.

"You left him!" Miss Donna assumes. "Thank you, Jesus!"

"Sort of but not the way you think," LaKeya says. "Booker, ah, Booker has died."

Miss Donna gasps and covers her mother.

"How?" she asks.

"He fell off a balcony," LaKeya says. "He was cheating on me, and he and his mistress were fighting, and she pushed him off the balcony."

"Oh my goodness!" Miss Donna says.

"Are you okay?" Mr. Jake asks.

"Ah, I guess. Still a bit numb and emotional."

"Where are the boys?" Miss Donna says. "They are in the guest room. I have been staying here since yesterday."

Miss Donna nods her head. LaKeya takes her parents to the guest room to meet their grandchildren. I look at Vision and Nathan.

"That wasn't so hard." Vision says.

"They're her parents, and as you can see, they were not too fond of Booker."

"Journ, come sit down," Nathan says, tapping the seat beside him.

I smile and sit next to him. He puts his arm around me, and he kisses me on the forehead.

"You have been so concerned about LaKeya that you haven't really taken care of yourself," Nathan said.

"I'm okay," I said.

"Excuse me; I am going to make some phone calls." Vision says. "I'll be in the office."

Vision walks out of the Great Room. I look at Nathan.

"I appreciate what you're doing and what you've done for LaKeya." I said to Nathan.

"As a matter of fact, you have been a great boyfriend, and you're not my boyfriend."

Nathan looks at me, his eyes intense yet soft.

"Not your boyfriend?" he asks.

"Not in so many words." I said, "Considering that this is just a vacational fling."

Nathan nods his head.

"You have a point," Nathan said. "However, I find myself liking you more than what time is permitting."

"Really?" I ask.

"Yes, there is something about you," Nathan said. "Like my sister, I followed your career. I thought it was cool when LaKeya informed me that she and you were good friends and you will be the godmother to the boys. Getting to know you these past few days, your love for your friend, your business sense, your style, everything about you, I like."

"So now what?"

"Maybe we can move forward and see where this goes. Maybe we cannot limit this to a summer thing." Nathan said. "Plus, my sister likes you."

"That's the deal-breaker," I joke.

Nathan chuckles.

"No, I make my own decisions, but her opinion means a lot," Nathan said.

LaKeya and her parents enter the Great Room. Miss Donna and Mr. Jake each carrying a baby in their arms. I can see that Miss Donna and LaKeya had been crying. Both Miss Donna and Mr. Jake sit down on the love seat.

"I made dinner, grilled salmon and vegetables," I said.

"I rather have a grilled T-Bone and bake potato."
Mr. Jake said.

Miss Donna chuckles and shakes her head.

"Jake," she admonishes.

"It's fine," I said, smiling. "The grill is still warm."

"I'm steak man myself," Nathan said, smiling. "I
can prepare you a nice steak, well done or-,"

"Yes, sir," Mr. Jake said smiling, "Well done."

Nathan smiles and gets up, and walks to the kitchen
to prepare the steak for Mr. Jake.
Miss Donna looks at Vision.

"My daughter has told me of your generosity and
kindness." Miss Donna said. "Thank you is not enough."

"It's perfectly fine, Mrs. Wilson." Vision says,
smiling. "I am happy to help."

"When is Booker's family coming?" Miss Donna
asks.

"Their jet lands tomorrow," I answer.

"What about the christening?" Miss Donna asks.

"Cancelled." LaKeya scoffs.

"Considering all that is going on, we still need to
lift these babies to the Lord." Miss Donna said.

"Maybe put something together with close friends
and family after the funeral," I suggest.

"I am not doing anything for Booker; let his family
deal with it." LaKeya scoffs, rolling her eyes.

"Keya, baby, that is not the right thing to do." Miss
Donna scolds softly. "He was still the boys' father."

LaKeya doesn't respond. She walks to the bay
window and looks at the view. I look at Miss Donna and
Mr. Jakes and shrug my shoulders.

"I wish things ended differently." Mr. Jake said.

Mr. Jake looks down at the baby and waves his hands at the baby. The baby moves his arms and coos at his grandfather. Mr. Jake smiles at the baby.

"He looks like me." Mr. Jake said proudly.

"They're identical, Jake." Miss Donna said. "Does that mean this one looks like you too?"

She asks, referring to the twin that she is holding.

"Yes," Mr. Jake said, smiling.

We laugh at Mr. Jake. If anything, the boys favor both LaKeya and Booker together.

WE SIT AND DINE. Wine, grilled seafood, grilled vegetables, and Mr. Jake and his baked potato and well done steak, we all ate dinner and talked about ways to move forward.

"We can move to Atlanta with us," Miss Donna said.

LaKeya nods her head. I can tell that Atlanta is not where she wants to be.

"I would rather stay in New York," LaKeya said.

"Keya baby," Mr. Jake says. "Atlanta will be better for you and the boys. A lot of our family is down there to help you."

"This is not supposed to be my life," LaKeya said. "You guys didn't raise me for this life."

"We raised you to be prominent, to be married to a good man, not to be a doormat." Miss Donna said. "I must admit that we were blinded by the financial security that Booker offered. We were not aware of the strings that were attached."

"What is to become of my boys now? They have no man to look up to."

"They have me," Nathan said. "Considering I am their godfather, or has that changed?"

"No, it hasn't changed," LaKeya said, touching Nathan's hand. "But your life is in New York. My parents are telling me to stay in Atlanta."

"Miss Donna and Mr. Jake, Nathan, and I will be there for LaKeya and the boys," I said.

"What are you going to do for work?" Mr. Jake asks. "You haven't worked since college."

"I don't know," LaKeya said. "I wasn't brought up to work."

Miss Donna tabs her eyes with her napkin.

"We made a mistake raising you," Miss Donna said. "Jake, we raised a princess-,"

"That kissed a frog." Mr. Jake scoffs.

"Mr. and Mrs. Wilson," Vision says. "If it's any consolation, my lawyers plan on making sure that LaKeya is well taken care of. She wouldn't have to work. She and the boys will be fine."

"You have that much pull against Booker's family." Miss Donna asks doubtfully.

"Oh yes." Vision said, putting a piece of grilled squash in her mouth. "I can see to it that LaKeya and the boys are well off also."

"Well," Mr. Jakes scoffs. "Must be nice to have money."

"It's not about money, Mr. Wilson," Vision said. "It's about angles."

"What is your real reason for helping my daughter?" Mr. Jake asks.

"Jake?" Miss Donna admonishes.

"No, seriously!" Mr. Jake said. "I don't mean any disrespect because we are grateful, but what are you getting out of this."

Vision glances at her brother. I know that she doesn't want to tell her truth. I don't want her to have to tell it because it's her issue.

"We are all friends, Mr. Wilson; that is all. If we can't help each other and rely on each other, then whom can we trust and rely on? Most communities, the Jewish, the Latinas, the Indians, all rally around each other being that support financially, mentally, and emotionally. However, the black culture doesn't have the same mind frame. We support biological family, and that's it. We have to learn to support one another."

"Hmph," Mr. Jake scoff. "You look white to me."

"Jake!" Miss Donna admonishes. "Miss Campbell, please forgive my husband."

"No apologies need, Mrs. Wilson." Vision said softly. "Mr. Wilson, despite my physical appearance, I am black."

Mr. Jake looks away, embarrassed by his comment.

"I'm sorry," he says humbly.

Vision nods her head, accepting his apology.

"Right now, we are on a roller coaster of emotion." Vision said. "Everything will be fine, I promise. Once Mr. and Mrs. Matthews get here, and after the funeral, things will fall into place."

Vision has a way of charming people. Her beauty somehow settled the brewing rage in Mr. Jake. I must admit, I am impressed. There is a power behind Vision that I am beginning to covet. I don't need her beauty; I like my chocolate brown skin. We both have our hair in dreadlocks. We both like designer clothes and we both have money.

However there is a power that she has that controls the atmosphere. What is the secret? The answer to that secret is what makes her a legend.

THE LOFT HAS AT three guest rooms. I assisted LaKeya with helping her parents get settled into one of the guest rooms. Mr. Jake is watching ESPN with Nathan, LaKeya, Miss. Donna and I assist with helping them unpack.

"So much for a vacation," LaKeya says sarcastically.

"It's all right, LaKeya." Miss Donna said. "Everything will be all right."

LaKeya shrugs her shoulders as she hangs her mother's dresses in the closet.

"Journey, how are things with you?" Miss Donna asks.

"Everything is going well," I said, smiling.

"Book sales are good?" Miss. Donna asks.

"Yes, going well," I said, smiling.

"Good, good girl," Miss Donna said, putting clothes into the drawer. "I am so glad that you girls stayed friends after all these years."

LaKeya and I look at each other and smile.

"Friends grow apart." Miss Donna said. "They grow up and start families, and life happens, and the next time we hear anything is that they had died, but you two remained friends, good friends."

"I am glad too," I said.

"You know Journey, your parents, Jake and myself, one day we sat down in the living room, I can't remember whose home, but we sat in the living room complaining about the neighborhood, about this and that and promised that you two girls would not live like we did. We promised to help each other with you two girls. If you Journey needed school clothes or supplies and Jake and I had the extra money, we brought them. Visa Versa for LaKeya, if there was a need for you; Journey's parents took care of it. We helped each other financially with bills, food; you name it; we did it for your girls. We were determined that you girls were going to not ever live in the projects. We worked long hours for someone; we wanted you, girls, to never work for anyone. Journey, I can speak for your parents when I saw

we are very proud of you. We are proud of all of your accomplishments."

I never knew of the information that Miss Donna shares. I knew LaKeya and my parents worked hard, but as far as relying on each other for money was news.

"Once you two started going your separate ways, I prayed that you girls still keep in touch and be there for one another if anything should happen. I am glad to see that you are here, Journey."

"I wouldn't have it any other way," I said to Miss Donna.

Miss Donna looks to LaKeya,

"If I had anything to do with this heartache, baby, I'm sorry."

"What, Mom, what do you mean?"

"Your father and I raised you to be that princess. You are our only child. Your daddy wanted you to marry a man that can do more for you than us; however, we did not want you to suffer because of our goals."

"Mommy, I made my bed; I have to lay in it," LaKeya said. "This is a humbling experience."

Miss Donna nods her head.

"The positive thing out of all this, we have two beautiful babies." Miss Donna says, smiling.

LaKeya doesn't comment.

THE LOFT IS QUIET, is well past midnight. Mr. Jake and Miss Donna are asleep. Nathan was actually asleep in the master bedroom, and Vision had left with the promise of returning tomorrow to help deal with Booker's parents. LaKeya and I sit on the patio drinking wine and nibbling on leftovers, and drinking wine.

There is a crescent moon in the ski. There are no clouds and no stars. The air is humid, just how I like it.

"Today has been rough," LaKeya says.

"Yeah," I said, sipping my drink.

"Everything is going to be okay," I said.

"Everyone keeps saying that," LaKeya said. "Eating the salmon."

"It will be," I said. "I promise."

"How are you so sure? Because the power of Vision Campbell says so?" LaKeya asks.

"No, because you don't nothing wrong, and no judge will allow Booker's parents to take the boys and for you not to get income as Booker's widow."

LaKeya shakes her head.

"Key, did you love Booker?" I ask

"Yes," LaKeya says quickly. "I love him; he has charisma. He had that swag. He promised me the world. Just be that woman on his arm, and I can have the world. Believe it or not, Journ, I didn't need the world. I just wanted him. Those nights, those quiet nights, we talk, laugh, talk about our dreams and goals, children."

I listen to her talk about her love for Booker.

"We wanted at least two," she chuckles. "Ironically, we had them at the same time."

"I know," I said, smiling. "Twins run in Book's family?"

LaKeya shakes her head.

"Nope, just a miracle," LaKeya says, smiling.

I smile and then eat a piece of salmon.

"I wanted to do a charity for inner-city children. Have a type of youth center, a place they can go after school when their parents weren't home. I wanted tutors, and people there that can help hone in hobbies, like writing, sewing, art." LaKeya said.

"Key," I said, impressed.

"I wanted to help make the neighborhood that we grew up in with neighborhood watch and recreating the homes," LaKeya said. "But to Booker, that wasn't good. Per him, we didn't need another youth center or neighborhood watch, and YouTube can teach people how to sew and draw. His family wanted me at their social events. I was to speak when spoken to. I was to not have an opinion, just sit, be pretty and be well-behaved."

I shake my head.

"My parents wanted me to marry rich, only because my dreams and goals did not assure me a comfortable lifestyle. Booker's family needed a beautiful woman on his arm. Considering that their bank is a family bank, they geared their attention to reputable families. Booker could not be a bachelor, one as a womanizer that looked bad, so Booker had to marry. He needed to marry someone light-skinned and beautiful. Ironically the fact that Vision Campbell didn't make the cut was shocking. I saw him at a party, a fundraiser for children with sickle cell. We made small talk about before I knew I was whisked in this world.

176

My ego made me stay. I was married to Booker Matthews, the world's most eligible black man. I enter a room, and people's eyes fixated on me. Journ, when we went to Christina's and Thom's and they noticed you over me. You are dark-skinned. You are rich and successful-,"

She stops talking and shakes her head.

"The jealousy that ran through me." She confesses. "That is not me. That is not us."

"It's okay," I said softly, tears fall from my eyes.

She looks at me. I quickly wipe my tears away. I didn't realize that her actions had hurt me so much.

"Journ, I am so sorry." LaKeya says softly.

Embarrassed by my tears, I look away. I forgive her. I really do. The weight of her apology has lifted from my shoulders.

"It's okay," I said, finally regaining my composure.

"What can I do to make this up to you?" LaKeya asks. "I'll do anything."

"Just realize who your true friends are," I said.

"I do," she says softly. "Light-skinned, dark-skinned, rich or poor

"Did you ever think that you can leave?" I ask.

"Where was I going to go? I had no money, and if I take the boys, it would be kidnapping. I was stuck in this marriage. I tried to be positive. When the boys came, I thought I could put my attention on them, but he and his family kept me from bonding with them."

"What? Why?" I ask, shocked.

"The boys are considered an asset. If they hate me or not feel anything for me, if anything was to happen, they can choose their father and not me. That is the real reason why I didn't breastfeed."

I shake my head at the idea.

"But I wanted to bond with my boys; I wanted them to smile when I enter the room."

"They do," I said.

"I know," LaKeya says with a smile. "I love the way they look at me when I feed them. It's as if they have eyes for only me."

I smile.

"When are you going to settle down and have a baby?" LaKeya asks.

I shrug.

"You still are not going to talk about Nathan?" she asks.

I shake my head. She lets out a sigh. I chuckle.

"Well, I am turning in," she says. "Got to get up early to face the devil."

I shudder at the idea of Booker's parents being called the devil. From what LaKeya has said of them, they are evil. She and I stand up, and we bid each other good night. I watch her walk back into the loft, and I sit down on the patio and look up at the heavens.

I think. So much has happened within the past week, just seven days. From arriving on this beautiful island to shopping and the world's most luxurious boutiques to defending my worth, my dark-skinned worth, and my economic status worth, and now burying my best friend's husband. There is Nathan, the perfect Island fling to now boyfriend. He has someone who captured me emotionally and, of course, physically. Nathan has introduced me to awesome people and opened my eyes to the politics of The Island, the Established and The New, light-skinned vs. dark-skinned.

In this world, I understand that this will be how things are. People will not like you because of their issues.

LaKeya was jealous of me because of my fame which knocked her off her pretty pedestal. However, considering what she was living with, she was more jealous of the freedom I have. I am not bound to an evil husband or his family. I don't have to ask for money. I can come and go as I please. I am beautiful and dark-skinned. I am famous by myself, not because of my association with anyone. Thom and Christina knew me because of my book sales because of the hard work that I have done.

I think of Vision Campbell. She seems like a very humble person. Her beauty is captivating, yet she doesn't use it to manipulate. She had allowed me to house LaKeya and her family in her loft, her house. She is willing to help LaKeya out of the pits of hell so she can live. I wonder what really happened with her and Booker's relationship. For her to use her beauty to haunt Booker and to create a world of revenge, she must have loved him. How was he when he was with her? Was he mean and controlling? I wonder that if Vision had married Booker, would she be in LaKeya's shoes? I nod my head, answering my question.

I think of the legend of Vision Campbell how she managed to recreate herself. When I think of all the images I have seen of her, they were all of her as a model, nothing from her younger days. Her background is a mystery. Nathan said that she is adopted. I am surprised that I never saw images with her and Nathan. I never saw a photo of her on the red carpet at some kind of Hollywood event or music industry party. I never saw her take photos with other famous people. The images of Vision that I have seen were just her, modeling in diamonds, fancy clothes, semi-nude. Her reclusive demeanor has created the idea that she is a myth, that she doesn't exist and only the selected few has seen her. I have never seen images of her with Booker;

then again, I wonder if his parents had anything to do with that thought.

How did she create this illusion? Just be reclusive? J. D. Salinger was reclusive, Howard Hughes was reclusive. Being reclusive is because they fear rejection, but who can reject Vision Campbell? Booker and his family, just like LaKeya, rejected me. Marcus rejected me too. The fear of rejection can be paralyzing. I know not being wanted by my silly boyfriends hurt me. I wonder was I not enough. Was I too dark-skinned or not skinny enough? At times doing a book signing or speaking engagement was a press because I wonder if I looked good. Will the people like what I am saying? Will they buy my book? Once they buy it, will they read it, will they like it. Rejection is powerful, and it can kill. However, to build a career off rejection is hard work because I had to not only get past the idea of not being wanted but to be presentable to those who may want me. There is the constant proving and validating one's self. Is that what Vision Campbell did?

She took rejection from both sides of the family, from her ex-husband and Booker, and created a kingdom that no one can conqueror. I don't have a reason to build such a kingdom, but I like the idea of owning a world like hers.

"Hey," I hear a voice.

I turn around and see Nathan. I smile at him.

"What are you doing up?" he asks, approaching me.

"LaKeya and I were out here talking, and I just stay back to enjoy the scenery," I said, smiling.

I stand up. Nathan kisses me on the lips. I missed his lips. Nathan sits down, and I sit on his lap. Nathan puts his arms around me.

"What are you thinking about?" he asks.

"A lot," I confess.

"Elaborate."

"I want to create a kingdom like your sister," I confess.

"Why?" Nathan asks.

"Because she is powerful," I said.

"Is that how you see things?" Nathan asks.

"I see her very successful. She has the liberty to do what she wants."

"So do you," Nathan said.

"Yes, but I still had to rent the loft. I want to own the loft. I want to own the islands, create a world so people like LaKeya and Vision won't suffer."

"Like Vision?" Nathan asks.

"I know you help brand her," I said, looking at him.

"How did you know that?" Nathan asks.

"Just a hunch," I answer. "You did well."

Nathan chuckles and pulls me closer to him to kiss me.

"Your sister is a legend, a myth," I said, smiling.

7

I INFORMED LEE TO have the Matthews come to the loft to meet with LaKeya regarding Booker. I wanted everything to be perfect for LaKeya, the less stress, the better for her. Nathan, Vision and I made sure there was plenty of food, from chicken to steak to seafood. I wanted to make sure that I was dressed properly. I found nice pair of white wide-leg slack and a white button-up silk blouse. I pinned my locks into a bun. I wore a pair of aquamarine-colored pearls and matching pearl studded earrings, and I wore gold high heel shoes. When Vision came, of course, she looked like a million dollars. She wore a black pair cigarette pants and a button-up royal blue blouse. In her ears are those emerald-cut diamond earrings. She wore her dreadlocks down. I was impressed with how long her dreadlocks were. She smiles at me when she enters the loft.

"You look beautiful." She compliments.

"Thank you, as you." I compliment back.

"Where is LaKeya?" Vision asks.

"She is getting dressed. She is a nervous wreck." Miss Donna says, entering the foyer. "Hello, Vision."

"Mrs. Wilson, hello."

Nathan enters the foyer. He looks handsome and comfortable with a pair of jeans and a button-up navy blue shirt.

"Dinner is ready whenever the Matthews get here.

"My husband is in the guest room with boys, just in case things get ugly." Miss Donna said.

LaKeya comes from the guest room. She looks beautiful wearing a soft pink pencil skirt and black silk boat neck shirt, and a pair of black Mary Jane high heel shoes.

"Hi," LaKeya says to Vision; she is smiling a nervous smile.

Vision walks to LaKeya and takes her hands.

"Everything is going to be okay." Vision says, smiling to her.

I see the limousine pulling up to the loft. The driver gets out of the car and opening the back door. I watch as what I assume Mrs. Matthews gets out of the car and then Mr. Matthews. I turn to face everyone. I watch LaKeya take in a deep breath and not exhale. Vision still stands next to LaKeya, holding her hand. I look at LaKeya; she nods her head. I open the door, and standing before me was Mr. and Mrs. Matthews. Without waiting for an invitation, they walk into the loft. I shut the door. I watch as they stare at LaKeya and Vision. I watch Vision stare at the Matthews with cool eyes, as if she doesn't have a care in the world.

I look at Mrs. Matthews. She actually is a very pretty, brown-skinned woman. She wears a black A-line style dress and a pair of pearls in her ears, and a pair of black low high heels. She had a small black leather purse, and she wore black gloves. She wore red lipstick. Her eyes were dark and penetrating. Her hair was short worn in tight curls. Mr. Matthews is handsome. He wears a navy blue suit, no tie. He has gray curly hair that is slick back, and he wears glasses; he too stars at Vision and LaKeya.

"Hello," LaKeya says.

Both Mr. and Mrs. Matthews nod their head slightly, acknowledging LaKeya. Vision says nothing.

They look at Miss Donna. Miss Donna looks at them with fire in her eyes. I look at Nathan. I take in a deep breath.

"Mr. and Mrs. Matthews, how about we sit down in the Great Room?" I suggest.

Mrs. Matthew turns her head slightly and looks at me.

"That be fine." Mr. Matthews said.

Nathan leads them to the Great Room. I shake my head. I know it's going to be a long evening.

In the Great Room, Mr. and Mrs. Matthews sit down on the one love seat. LaKeya and Miss Donna sit on the couch. Nathan, Vision, and I sit on the other love seat. For a long minute, no one knows how to begin. Who starts to talk? I do.

"Mr. and Mrs. Matthews, I like to start off by saying how sorry I am for your loss," I say.

"LaKeya, explain to Mr. Matthews and me what happened." Mrs. Matthews required.

I look at LaKeya; she takes in a deep breath. She looks at Mr. and Mrs. Matthews.

"Booker's mistress pushed him off the balcony," LaKeya says coolly.

"Who was she?" Mrs. Matthews asks.

"Monica," LaKeya answers.

"Monica, who?" Mrs. Matthews questions.

"Barnes." LaKeya answers.

"How in the world did she manage to push my son off the balcony?" Mrs. Matthews questions as if LaKeya is telling a lie.

"They were fighting." LaKeya answers.

"I suggest you elaborate, girl." Mr. Matthews demands. "I can have you charged for murder."

"You will do no such thing." Vision says coolly.

"Who are you to speak, mutt!" Mr. Matthews snaps.

Quickly Nathan stands up.

"I am the woman that will own you." Vision says, coolly.

"Hey, hey!" I stand up. "Arguing and name calling is not going to help! A life is gone; a son, a husband, has died."

It's quiet for a moment, but the tension is very, very thick.

"May get anyone anything to drink?" I ask.

Several head shakes declining drinks. I shrug my shoulders.

"Mr. and Mrs. Matthews, I had meet Monica, and it was not a pleasant experience," I said. "I also witness Booker insult LaKeya just two days ago. All due respect, your son had a very tainted way of dealing with people."

"How dare you?" Mrs. Matthews hissed.

I shrug my shoulders unapologetically.

"You killed my son." Mrs. Matthews said to LaKeya.

"Your son got what he deserves!" LaKeya snaps.

"Keya!" Miss Donna admonishes.

"No," LaKeya rebukes her mother. "You and your son are manipulative and hurtful. Your son was having an affair in our bed in a room adjacent to our children, with a woman that you yourselves promised me was not a treat! She took it upon herself to try to kill Booker and me in the same house that your grandsons were in! How dare you accuse me of killing him?!"

"Where is he?" Mr. Matthews asks.

"He is in the Island Morgue." LaKeya answers.

"Where is Monica?" Mrs. Matthews asks.

"In police custody," LaKeya responds.

"Where are the twins?" Mr. Matthews asks.

I am sitting across from LaKeya, and I felt her heart jump.

"Can we see them?" Mrs. Matthews asks.

"No," LaKeya says.

"Keya, maybe you should-," Miss Donna says softly.

"No," LaKeya shakes her head." No. Not until I get in writing and notarized that you will try to take them from me."

"We have a right to our grandchildren." Mrs. Matthews states.

"And I have a right to protect my children, and I don't think you suitable to be in their lives." LaKeya states.

I sit on the couch, proud of her. I fight to keep from smiling. I watch as Mr. and Mrs. Matthews take in a deep breath.

"You won't collect a dime of our money." Mr. Matthews states cruelly. "We worked too hard to lose and give our money away to the likes of you."

"Mr. Matthews," Miss Donna says. "I dare not sit here and allow you to insult my daughter. It is no secret that the Matthews' Empire is wicked and mean, but the Wilson Empire can be just as mean. Now my husband and I watch for at least five years how your son mentally and emotionally abused my child, and Mrs. Matthews, I am sure as a mother you don't take too kindly to your children being hurt, hence your demeanor now. The issue is your son, got caught and now he is dead."

I see tears welling up in Mrs. Matthews' eyes. She takes in a deep breath, reaches into her purse and pulls out a handkerchief, and dabs away her tears.

"A man's actions have cost him his life, regardless of the type of man he is. You lost a child. I suggest we sit down and discuss how to move forward." Miss Donna says.

"That is easy for you to say, you have your child; we don't have ours." Mrs. Matthews says.

"I'm sorry." Miss. Donna said.

"I am not participating in a funeral," LaKeya said. "I won't give you that satisfaction."

"We're leaving." Mr. Matthews abruptly stands up.

Mrs. Matthews stands up as well. I stand with the attempt to walk them out, but Mr. Matthews puts his hand up, rejecting.

"Don't bother!" he hisses.

We watch them walk out the Great Room, through the foyer, and out the door, slamming the door. I look at LaKeya. She finally breaks. She covers her face and cries. Her mother puts her arms around her comforting her.

"The hard part is over." Vision says softly. "My lawyers are ready in case they try something.

LaKeya sits up she wipes her tears away. I nod my head at her.

"You did good." I said, smiling. "You did real good."

"Let's eat," Nathan said.

We walk into the dining room. Miss Donna goes to the guest room to get Mr. Jake and the boys. Together we sit down at the dining table. I smile at the spread of food and the wine on ice. Nathan has set a beautiful table. For what seems like ten minutes, everyone piled food on their plates or passed food around from one person to another. This was more than just dinner with friends but a celebration. LaKeya stood up to her Mr. and Mrs. Matthews. We know that she will be able to raise her boys without any emotional hindrances.

"I like to make a toast," I said, standing up.

I raised my glass everyone raises their glasses with me.

"I like to toast to friendship and family. It warms my heart to see how this family rallied around LaKeya during this horrific ordeal. It warms my heart that Vision and Nathan have assisted as well. Your act of kindness has taken a heavy weight off my sister's shoulders. She can raise her sons in peace, to friendship!"

"To friendship!" everyone says, toasting.

I sit down and resume eating the delicious meal that Nathan has prepared.

THE NEXT MORNING, I wake to find LaKeya in the breakfast nook. Miss Donna had cooked a big breakfast. There was bacon, eggs, home fries, sausages, waffles. Fresh fruit had been set out on the table.

"Morning, Miss Donna," I said smiling.

"Morning, baby." She replies, smiling.

I lean forward and kiss her on the cheek.

"How did you sleep?" Miss Donna asks.

"I slept well, you?" I ask.

"I slept well. Jake has taken the boys for a walk around the block. I cannot believe at how beautiful The Island is."

"Oh yes!"

"Is this your first time here?" Miss Donna asks.

"Yes, ma'am," I answer.

I pour myself a cup of coffee and then take a sip. I chuckle at myself.

"What?" I ask with a smile.

"I remember when you started drinking coffee; remember how your mother used to get so mad at you for drinking coffee."

"Yes," I said, smiling. "Then she got the coffee maker, and I didn't know how to use it. She wanted me to make her a pot, she reluctantly showed me, and whenever she would ask me to make her a pot, I would steal a cup, and then eventually she would finally say; 'Make us some coffee,'"

"Yes," Miss Donna chuckles. "But you were fourteen years old drinking coffee. What did you know about coffee?"

"Sophisticated people drank coffee," I said, smiling. "You and Mother would look like those women from *Dynasty*. Ms. Dianne Carroll, looking regal and classy, you and Mommy would sit at the table drinking coffee, eating coffee cake, and discussing important matters. You look sophisticated."

"We sat and caught up on our stories," Miss Donna confesses with a laugh. "Remember I told you we took care of each other. Even with our stories, if I missed an episode of Erica Kane causing trouble and your mother saw it, she filled me in."

I laugh at how in tune my mother and Miss Donna had been.

"You and my mother were the best of friends," I said.

"As Mr. Jake and your father. We have to stay together in order to survive that neighborhood. I miss those days."

"I'm sure they miss those days too. I want to thank you and Mr. Jake for doing what you have done for me as I grew up."

"Thank you for helping LaKeya." Miss Donna said. "I know things had been strained, she can always be a bit stiff, but I know that she loves you."

I smile.

"Where is she?" I ask.

"In the breakfast nook." Miss Donna answers.

I nod my head and walk into the breakfast nook. I see LaKeya sitting at the table, looking out the window; the pretty candy-colored birds fly around. She turned to me; she smiles at me. I smile at her. She looks rested, as beautiful as she had looked when I first arrive on The Island.

"Good morning," I said.

"Good morning," she says to me.

"Your mother made an amazing breakfast," I said.

"I know, but I am not really hungry."

"You okay?" I ask, sitting down at the table.

"Yes." She said. "I was thinking of leaving The Island today and go back to New York."

"Really?" I said. "You really don't want to assist with Booker's funeral? I mean, despite him being who he is, he is still the boys' father."

LaKeya shrugs.

"I know that there is will a media storm when I get back to the States. I need to get my head together because of course, it's going to look like I did it or done something; caused something."

"That is why you cannot ignore his funeral," I said.

"I am going to tell the truth; his mistress killed him. I will not say her name and go into a quiet life with my sons and me."

I sigh. By the look on LaKeya's face, she is serious. There is nothing I can do or say to make her feel better.

"Is there anything I can do?" I ask.

"Pay for the plane fare." She says coolly.

I nod my head, knowing that I would be anyway.

"Morning," Nathan says, entering the breakfast nook.

"Good morning, Nathan." Both LaKeya and I say, smiling.

"LaKeya is thinking about leaving today," I inform.

"Okay," Nathan says, "I can have Vision charter her jet and get you and your family home."

"You have done more than enough, Nathan." LaKeya, says smiling.

"It's nothing, really," Nathan said.

VISION CAMPBELLS' PRIVATE JET was ready for LaKeya and her family within an hour. I was not surprised yet taken back. She also had set up a car to be available when LaKeya is ready to go to the airport and a car waiting for them when the jet lands. LaKeya didn't hesitate to get ready and to go back with her parents back to New York. So I assisted LaKeya, and her parents pack their bags and the boys and prepare to leave.

"What about you?" Nathan asked me,

"I think I should go to. Maybe assist with LaKeya clean up the mess back in New York." I said.

Nathan nods his head. He looked somewhat sad.

"Don't look so sad," I said.

"Maybe next week we can meet up for a drink and resume our Island Romance." He suggests.

"I like that," I said, smiling.

Nathan leans down and kisses me passionately. I melt in his arms.

"Nathan, this past week has been the best week I had in a long time. Thank you so much for being here for my friend and me."

He leans forward and kisses me again. I step back, and he takes my hands and kisses them.

8

AS PREDICTED, THERE IS a firestorm of media and paparazzi standing outside my apartment, waiting for some kind of answer. The limousine pulls up to my apartment, and I see photographers all waiting to get some information on the death of Booker Matthews. LaKeya, her parents get out of the limousine carrying the boys in their car seats.

"Please back up," I requested, trying to be some kind of guard to them.

"LaKeya, LaKeya," they call out her name.

The camera is flashing. I am glad that we covered the boys' faces. I watch as Mr. Jake and Miss Donna cover their eyes.

We manage to get into the apartment. We went into my Great Room. Mr. and Miss Donna sit down on the couch as I look out the window and see the mass of people surrounding the front waiting for sight or a glimpse of answers.

LaKeya sets the boys' car seats down on the floor. I watch as LaKeya eyes scan my Great Room. I watch her take in what she sees. I have every one of my book covers in a frame mounted on the wall. She walks through my home. I follow her. On the walls are photos of me posing with celebrities that I met at book signings. I take her to my office. My office is black and white, white walls with a desk the color of ebony wood desk, a computer and printer, bookshelves, and a fax machine. Also on the walls are pictures of me and my books. Her eyes look as if she has never seen any like this before.

"Amazing," she says softly.

"What's amazing?" I ask.

"The life you have created." She said.

I shrug my shoulders, indicating that it was nothing, but I know it was hard work. I pick up my phone and dial the manager's office.

"Yes," I hear the manager say.

"Hi, it's Journey Calloway; there is a swarm of people outside harassing my guest and me. Is it possible to have them removed?"

"Sure, I will have them removed immediately, Ms. Calloway."

"Thank you."

I hang up the phone.

"Looks like you're the new Vision Campbell," LaKeya says.

"What do you mean?"

LaKeya chuckles.

"Look at this world you created?" LaKeya said.

"Vision created a world to get back at Booker,"

"She created a world to show ignorant-minded that she didn't come to play," LaKeya said. "Look at this empire you created, Journ."

I looked around at the photos on the walls, the luxury apartment that I live in. I shrugged my shoulders, indicating that it wasn't much.

"Your humility is empowering," LaKeya said. "Vision created her table, and that is what you did! The legend is more than a pretty face; it's establishing your worth to those who won't see you naturally, so you make them see you, mentally and financially. I had to see you, they see you."

I nodded my head understanding what LaKeya was saying.

"I'm ready to build my table," LaKeya said.

"I see you," I said, smiling.